Alumni Association Toronto Baptist College

# Memoir of Daniel Arthur McGregor

Late Principal of Toronto Baptist College. Second Edition

Alumni Association Toronto Baptist College

**Memoir of Daniel Arthur McGregor**
*Late Principal of Toronto Baptist College. Second Edition*

ISBN/EAN: 9783337019211

Printed in Europe, USA, Canada, Australia, Japan

Cover: Foto ©Raphael Reischuk / pixelio.de

More available books at **www.hansebooks.com**

# MEMOIR

OF

# DANIEL ARTHUR MCGREGOR

LATE PRINCIPAL

OF

TORONTO BAPTIST COLLEGE

---

Published by the Alumni Association of
Toronto Baptist College

---

SECOND EDITION.

---

TORONTO:

DUDLEY & BURNS, PRINTERS

1891

Could I have said while he was here,
" My love shall now no further range ;
There cannot come a mellower change,
For now is love mature in ear."

Love then had hope of richer store ;
What end is here to my complaint?
This haunting whisper makes me faint,
" More years had made me love thee more.

But death returns an answer sweet :
" My sudden frost was sudden gain,
And gave all ripeness to the grain
It might have drawn from after-heat."

# PREFACE.

‑‑‑

THE Alumni Association of Toronto Baptist College, at its annual meeting in April 1890, decided to undertake the preparation and publication of a Memoir of Principal McGregor, then recently deceased. It was resolved to raise by subscription such a sum as would, when added to a small amount in the treasury of the Association, defray all the expenses of publication, and to bestow upon Mrs. McGregor the entire proceeds of the sale of the book. For the carrying out of this undertaking two committees were appointed : an Editing Committee, consisting of Professors Newman and Campbell, and a Finance Committee, consisting of Rev. W. C. Weir and Rev. J. L. Gilmour.

After a few months of joint effort on the part of the Finance Committee, the removal of Mr. Weir to a distant Province left the chief financial responsibility on Mr. Gilmour's shoulders. By dint of well directed and persistent effort the needful amount of money has been secured, and arrangements have been made, which, it is expected, will result in the prompt sale of the entire edition. To those who have generously contributed to the publishing fund the thanks of the Association and of the Denomination are due.

As the work of editing was not very burdensome and was scarcely susceptible of advantageous division, most of it naturally devolved upon the first-named member of the committee. Professor Campbell was frequently consulted as to the general features of the book; but he cannot fairly be held responsible for the execution of the editorial task. The committee decided at the outset to adopt the co-operative plan in the preparation of the biographical sketch, as likely to secure the best results, with the least delay and the least expenditure of individual effort. Rev. Malcolm MacGregor, of New York, the eldest brother of Principal McGregor, cheerfully undertook and faithfully, lovingly and ably executed the task of preparing Chapters I. and V. Chapter II. was assigned to Rev. E. W. Dadson, whose long acquaintance with Principal McGregor and his profound admiration for his character enabled him to write sympathetically and intelligently of the period of his life under consideration. Chapter III. was written by Rev. D. G. Macdonald, who as a student came to know and to love Principal McGregor, and as the beloved and efficient pastor of the Stratford church was in a position to judge of his work as a pastor and to exhibit this portion of his life in its true setting and its true light.

To Mrs. McGregor more than to any other individual are any excellencies that the memoir may possess due. She not only aided in the selection and securing of writers, but she furnished each writer with much valuable material and many valuable suggestions, and carefully examined the various chapters before they were given to the printer. To her also is due the selection of materials for Chapter VI. and the selection for publication of the essays, addresses, sermons, etc., contained in Part II. In an important sense she may be regarded as the Editor of the book.

The work of all, whether in collecting or contributing money, in furnishing materials, in writing, or in editing, has been from first to last a labor of love. That the little book may be a means of keeping fresh in the memory of our Canadian Baptists the life and work of one of the noblest and most Christlike of men, and thus of advancing in some humble measure the kingdom of Christ, is the earnest desire of all who have had to do with its publication.

# CONTENTS.

## PART I.

## PART II.

# PART I.

# BIOGRAPHICAL SKETCH.

# CHAPTER I.

A D. 1847-'70.

In undertaking, at the request of those having the matter in charge, to write certain chapters in the volume to be prepared and published in memory of DANIEL A. McGREGOR, it is with the utmost diffidence and shrinking of heart that his eldest brother, intimately associated with him through many changeful years, addresses himself to the unlooked-for, delicate and painful task. Perhaps, in the circumstances, a direct and familiar method of narration may, on the whole, embarrass the writer less and serve the purposes of the story more.

Whenever the character and life of a departed person become matters of general interest, there is invariably a desire to know something of his ancestry, however undistinguished, and of his surroundings, however common-place—such is mankind's instinctive recognition of the significance both of heredity and of environment in the development of individual human

A

life.   As, in this instance, the later ancestry and the
earlier surroundings are considerably interwoven with
important threads of the Baptist history of the Ottawa
Valley, some reference to them may not be undesi-
rable.

Both the parents of the subject of this memoir were
of Scottish birth.   As certain family traditions and
heir-looms attest, the line of his paternal ancestors
descended from him who, after the Gaelic manner,
was called "The Man of Royston"—Crag Royston
near Ben and Loch Lomond, in the hereditary lands
of the "Clan MacGregor": that is, the line descended
from the "Rob Roy MacGregor" of whom Sir Walter
Scott, in his way of mingling history and fiction, has
so vividly and entertainingly written.   In the latter
part of the last century, Daniel's paternal great-grand-
father, Robert, removed from Crag Royston to Glen
Lyon, where, in allusion to his business pursuits, he
was long and honorably known, in Gaelic phrase, as
Robert the merchant.   It was here and about 1809
that Robert's second son, Malcolm, married Miss Christian Blaikie, who, about the year 1816, was converted
to Christ, baptized upon profession of faith, and united
to the then infant Baptist church in Glen Lyon, which
sprang into existence directly or indirectly through
the evangelical movement originated and sustained
by the Haldane brothers.   Thus early was this family
brought into contact with spiritual Christianity and
New Testament Church principles; and greatly blessed
through many after years was the influence of her
whose heart and life were then consecrated to the

Saviour; and long will she be remembered as "a mother in Israel" and as a fervent lover of Christ and of souls.

In 1817, this wedded pair, with the four children born to them in Scotland, (the second of whom was Alexander, the future father of Daniel), left the land of their birth, for Canada, the land of their adoption, and spent the first three years after their arrival in Montreal. At some point in this period of time, the first Baptist communion service ever held in that city was observed in their house. On leaving Montreal the family moved up into the northern side of the Ottawa Valley and settled on a "forest farm" in the "Rear of Chatham" in the County of Argenteuil, where their children increased to the number of twelve, of whom four sons and four daughters are still living. Here settled also a number of other Scottish families from the neighborhood of Glen Lyon,—the McPhails, the McArthurs, the McGibbons, the McFarlanes, the McCallums and others. The renewal of old acquaintanceship in a new land, and in circumstances sometimes of peculiar hardship, was exceedingly grateful and helpful to all concerned. A Baptist church, of primitive type and spiritual tone, afterwards known as the Dalesville Church, was speedily formed, of which Duncan McPhail, a man "mighty in the Scriptures" and who had studied for a time under the Haldanes in Edinburgh, was the founder and leader, and informally the pastor; and through the efforts of himself and the brotherhood generally, the church grew in knowledge and in grace and was privileged to bring a goodly number of people to Christ, among whom were the pastor's son, Daniel McPhail, afterwards for the third of a century a singularly devoted and fruitful minister of the New Testament, Mrs. MacArthur, mother of the gifted and successful Dr. R. S. MacArthur, and Mr. McCallum, grandfather of the McEwens, well and favorably known in the Canadian Baptist ministry.

About the year 1834, the Breadalbane church, of which the future veteran Rev. William Fraser was pastor, was blessed, after a long and discouraging season of barrenness, with an extensive and glorious revival. In the good work the pastor was greatly assisted by Rev. John Gilmour of Montreal, whose own field of labor was visited a little later with copious showers of refreshing. The Dalesville church had given itself to prayer for a similar work of grace, and upon its earnest request Mr. Gilmour went in the winter of 1835 to its assistance. Here also he conducted a series of religious meetings through which a great number of people were brought to the Saviour, baptized, and added to the church. Among the converts of that time were Malcolm McGregor, ever after known as a noble and fruitful Christian, and all his older children, including Alexander, subsequently the father of Daniel. The personal influence and importunate prayers of Mrs. Malcolm McGregor were largely instrumental in the conversion of her husband and children.

Some few years after the Dalesville revival, Alexander McGregor, moved by the desire of doing more

efficient work for Christ, and influenced by the counsel of several brethren, including his pastor Rev. John
Edwards then settled in Dalesville, became a student
in the Montreal Baptist College, with the intention of
preparing himself, if so it might be, for the work of
the gospel ministry.   After about two years of successful study, though possessed of naturally vigorous
and fertile powers of mind, he desisted from the pro-
ject and turned to other pursuits, fearing that he
would be unable to overcome a partly constitutional
hesitancy of speech. From these circumstances he was
led in after life, when father of a family, to make it
habitually a matter of earnest secret prayer that it
might please God to call some of his sons into the
ministry in his stead—as anciently He had appointed
Solomon to erect the temple which David had not
been permitted to build.

On the same day, early in February 1842, that
Catherine his eldest sister was married to Rev. Daniel
McPhail, Alexander McGregor was united in marriage, at the same place, Dalesville, and by the same
minister, Rev. John Edwards, to Miss Clementine
McArthur, then of Montreal.  She was born in 1815,
in Glen Lyon, Scotland, and was the daughter of
Daniel McArthur, a man of sincere and ardent piety,
who took a deep interest in vital Christianity and in
the work of Christian missions then being prosecuted
in Scotland under the Haldanes and others ; and,
though he was a member and a precentor in the Pres-
byterian church, he manifested a great and tender
regard for the little Baptist church in his neighbor-

hood, often throwing open his house for its meetings. Had his life not been cut off prematurely, he would in all likelihood have united himself with this body of Christians, which was greatly to his mind; but before Clementine, his only daughter then surviving, was eight years old, he passed away from earth in the triumph of faith, to be followed in like manner a few years later by his widow. With her only surviving near relatives, her brother and her grand-uncle, Clementine came, when about sixteen years of age, to Montreal, where, under the ministry of Rev. John Gilmour, she was converted, baptized and united to the Baptist church; and it was there, during his student days, that she first made the acquaintance of her future husband. Through all her career subsequent to her conversion, till her blissful departure from this life, August 20th 1876, she was a spiritually-minded and tenderly conscientious Christian. For cheerful courage amid the disappointments and ills of life, and for gentleness and fervent good-will toward every one, she was remarkable; while for loving and whole-souled devotion to the best interests of the children whom God had given her, she was unexcelled.

Immediately after their marriage, Mr. and Mrs. Alexander McGregor went to the township of Osgoode and there for some six years settled upon a forest farm. In 1848 they moved away from Osgoode, and —as the husband's various pursuits, school-teaching, lumbering, milling and farming, required—lived successively in Dalesville, Rigaud, Lochiel, Breadalbane, Duncanville, Winchester, returning in 1860 to Osgoode where they remained till several years after Daniel left home to study for the ministry. In all, seven children were born to them, the third of whom died in infancy. Daniel was born December 13th, 1847, during the first residence in Osgoode, and was the younger of twin brothers and the fifth child in the family. During child-life, though not very robust, he was quite healthy, having no illness but a single short and sharp attack of fever from which he quickly recovered. In more advanced boyhood and in early manhood he developed an excellent physique and great muscular strength. In the mill, in the forest, on the farm, and on the lumber-laden streams, he had up to and including his twenty-second year his full share of arduous toil, attended at times with more than ordinary privations.

Among Daniel's characteristics there were several real, yet sufficiently consistent contrasts, which were perceptible in early life and which developed themselves strikingly through his maturer years. He was deferential yet independent; diffident yet determined. He enjoyed solitude; and he loved society. He was quite indisposed to tolerate unwarranted encroachments upon his personal rights; and he was in a remarkable degree self-sacrificing and chivalrous in the interests of others. He was so tender-hearted that, without some practical object in view he could scarcely even bear to hear recitals of suffering; but he could endure suffering itself with exemplary fortitude, whenever the providence of God demanded, and even inflict it, with a degree of unction, when persuaded that the

claims of justice and order required.   He had native
to him a faint tinge of melancholy, a slightly plain-
tive air, and a ready sympathy with things solemn
and awe-inspiring; and yet, though not exceptionally
witty himself, nor much the occasion of wit in others,
he had an exquisite sense and a hearty appreciation
of both wit and humor, severely governed, however,
by considerations of time and place.   Like the alter-
nations of major and minor strains in certain forms
of Celtic music, the modulations of his temperament,
which was essentially Celtic, often produced quite
varied and interesting effects.

Until after he was twenty-two years of age Daniel's
opportunities for attending school were few and unimportant, amounting in all, after his twelfth year, to
but a few weeks.   But though he was at so critical a
period, through force of circumstances, largely de-
prived of school advantages, he developed a keen taste
for reading and made himself thoroughly acquainted
with the contents of all manner of books within his
reach in private and circulating libraries.   For many
years, at night, and during intermissions of physical
toil, he studied the English poets earnestly and with
great relish.   It was long the practice of himself and
his younger brother, at intervals in the labors on
the farm and in the forest, to compete with each other
in reciting the poems, or in repeating the substance of
books which they had been reading aloud to each
other the evening before.   In these ways Daniel's
memory, and his mental powers generally, were greatly
quickened and strengthened; and he thus acquired a

mass of general information, which, when he became a college student, was recognized as exceptionally extensive and valuable, and which in after life was often of great service to him. His memory was stored in the same way with the gems of the British poets, especially those of Tennyson, whose density of thought and delicacy of diction had great attraction for him and greatly influenced his literary taste and feeling through all his after life.

It seems appropriate at this point to remark, for the encouragement of the young readers of this narrative, that a mind animated by the noble desire of self-improvement and of becoming useful in the world may find implements and opportunities always and everywhere; and that by suppressing all inordinate desire for amusements and trivial gratifications, and using diligently whatever fragments of time and means are available one may come in the course of years to possess mental power, discriminating taste, extensive knowledge, practical wisdom, and, if consecrated to Christ, capacity to serve efficiently God and humanity.

In order to indicate the type of Daniel's conversion and religious character, it will be helpful to refer for a moment to certain important religious influences that came upon him from the past and from his surroundings at the time of his becoming a Christian. The great revivals in Breadalbane, Dalesville and Montreal, from 1834 to 1836, in which his father and mother, then unknown to each other, were converted, were of such a powerful and radical nature that they

determined the general type of all the religious work
done subsequently among the Baptists in the Ottawa
Valley. Unquestioning deference towards the word
of God, profound conviction of sin, much awe of the
sterner aspects of the character and law of God, adoring and trustful recognition of the person and work
of Christ, reverential regard for the Holy Spirit's personality and influence, and an emotional experience
as intense and tender as it was unostentatious and
self-contained,—such were the characteristics which
according to all competent testimony, strongly pre-
dominated in that early religious movement, and
which have to this day plainly perpetuated themselves, in a remarkable degree, in those and in neighboring communities.

It was during this revival period in Dalesville,
though he was previously converted and accustomed
to address religious assemblies, that young Daniel
McPhail, now of blessed memory, developed that marvellous intensity and power of spirit, in gospel work,
which afterwards characterized him as a Christian
minister and made him the Elijah of the Ottawa Valley, where, employing the church in Osgoode, of which
he was pastor for twenty-seven years, as an operating
centre, he was privileged to see greatly multiplied,
through the blessing of God upon his labors, converts,
churches and recruits for the ministry, largely after
his own type. In close association with him in the
great work done in his day in various parts of that
religiously favored region, were several singularly
excellent and loyal ministers of the gospel — the

sturdy and faithful John King, the gentle and genial John Edwards, now in glory, the enthusiastic and fiery John Dempsey, the loving and kindly William K. Anderson, and, for a shorter and at an earlier period, the noble-hearted Robert A. Fyfe, afterwards through long years of varied and self-sacrificing toil till the hour of his untimely decease, the Moses of the Baptist denomination in Canada. The labors of this evangelical "band of brothers" were the means under God of setting up a standard of Christian piety singularly lofty, and of developing a type of Christian character of the rarest excellence. In the Osgoode, Ormond, and West Winchester churches, which for so long a period shared the pastoral care and evangelistic labors of Mr. McPhail, there came to be a large number of persons whose minds were fairly saturated with gospel truths and principles, and whose influence in their respective communities was of the very strongest and best.

Under such influences, converging upon him from the home, the social life, the church services, and from the personality of his uncle, Pastor McPhail, Daniel's earlier religious convictions and aspirations were formed; and to his latest day they largely determined his ideals of Christian excellence and of the kind of young men to be prayed for, sought out, and trained for the gospel ministry. When about twelve years of age he was the subject of very deep and tender religious impressions, which, though, they did not at the time issue in assured faith in Christ, lingered on for some seven years, neither permitting him the dead indifference of the worldling nor yielding him the living hope and joy of the Christian.

Early in the summer of 1867 he was very desirous of becoming a true Christian, but he almost despaired of ever finding the way to attain to that end.    On Sunday, June 16th, of that year, he had been wishing that some one would come and explain to him clearly the way of salvation.    That evening, the writer, then a student-preacher on a neighboring field, came, after his day's labor, and spent that balmy summer night with him in the open air, unfolding to him the way of life and persuading him to trust in Jesus.  Daniel's principal difficulty, like that of many other religious inquirers, arose from regarding emotional experiences instead of gospel declarations, invitations and promises, as the true warrant for faith in Christ.    But about the break of day there came day-break into his soul, and he believed on Christ for salvation because of His character, work and word.    In after years Daniel became very skilful in dealing with inquirers beset with the same or kindred difficulties; and the experience of that night has often helped the writer, furnishing him with a convincing instance and illustration, when endeavoring to induce inquirers similarly perplexed to surrender themselves trustingly and unconditionally to Christ.

Daniel's twin brother, Robert, having found the Saviour a few weeks later—on Sunday, August 25th —they were both baptised on the following Sunday afternoon, September 1st, in the Castor River, by Rev. P. G. Robertson, who, as the successor of Rev. D.

McPhail, was having, at the time, a season of reaping on the Osgoode field.

During the next three years Daniel made commendable progress in Christian knowledge, character and consecration; and after much exercise of soul and much counsel from worthy brethren as to whether he should devote himself to the work of the ministry, he came to the conclusion that, through the voice of his own heart and the voice of the Christian brotherhood, he was called of God—speaking through them and him—to labor in that vocation. Accordingly, in September, 1870, with the cordial recommendation of the Osgoode church, of which he was a member, he left his father's home for Woodstock, there to pursue studies preparatory for his life-work.

Other hands will trace the story of his life as a student, as a pastor, and as a theological professor, when it will remain for the present writer to give some account of his last illness.

# CHAPTER II.

Before saying anything of his education proper it
will be well to note some features of that earlier
drill which in almost every case has so powerful an
influence upon after life and which generally lies
at the foundation of one's education. Most men of
any note in the world can point back to certain circumstances in early life, and name them as the chief
factors of their after achievement. Mr. McGregor
could do so. He recognized very clearly, as did others,
that whatever attainments he made in his after career
began long before he had any thought of a technical
education, and in a school which if not famous in the
opinion of the schoolmen has nevertheless a record
in the practical world to which very few of the
learned institutions have attained. Ancestry counts
for something as an educative force, but he who can
trace to himself a clear strain of ancestral intellectualism, good judgment and common sense, may know
that he has something to thank besides the schools
for what advances he may have made. Mr. McGregor
had this derived intellectualism in good measure. His
father is known to the older men in our ministry as a

sound theologian whose course at the Montreal College manifested brain power, and whose subsequent
life has been one of thoughtfulness. Those who knew
his mother knew a woman of very superior excellence,
whose chief characteristic was strong common sense;
and this, prominent in a disposition marked by unusual tenderness and full-measured love, could not fail
in leaving the strong impressions it did upon her son.
Whatever he was as to heart, mind, or body, he was a
man preëminently of strong common sense. Some
features of his intellectual life may then be said to
have been inherited.

But intellectual or moral force thus had, every one
knows, is not necessarily retained. Indeed it vanishes
easily and early unless it be specially conserved.
Young McGregor's life was thrust into surroundings
which providentially were best fitted to preserve his
native endowments, and strengthen them. The family
consisted, besides the parents, of four boys and two
girls, and these all having upon them the same ancestral marks, became in themselves a school in which
intellectual and moral drill of no mean order was
daily exercised. Often have I heard from D. A.'s lips
the story of the mother influence and the paternal
example, the process of wit-sharpening indulged in
throughout the family circle, and his estimate of the
value of the home schooling.

But perhaps the schooling which most affected his
whole career was the character of the Osgoode environment in which his early life was passed. The
Osgoode Baptist Church and its revered pastor, Rev.

Daniel McPhail, have had upon the Canadian Baptist denomination, and upon Baptists elsewhere also, an influence which, though perhaps unknown to many, is nevertheless even to-day at work. Out of that church and from the influence of one of the most saintly men God ever gave to the churches, Osgoode men have preached the gospel throughout Ontario for the last thirty years. A remarkable people were the Osgoode church at the time of which we write. Scotch to a man, and theologians all, God and the Bible were the first thought throughout the community—or that part of it at least which threw its influence over young McGregor. The street-corner gathering as likely as not discussed points in theology in preference to horse-flesh. Every dinner table was a theological class, and with the pork and potatoes went Calvinism and Arminianism in due course. The Bible was the family hand-book, and, handled reverently, it was the arbiter of the daily discussion. How the old men loved the book, and how the youngsters had it heaped into them, pressed down, and running over, with porridge-and-milk regularity. And this was characteristic not of a few families but of the church, so that there was no escaping God and the Bible in that community. And what shall be said of the influence of the pastor, the man who went in and out of these homes, who served them their daily portion of spiritual meat, who directed their discussions and led them in their searching of the word of God, who was the constant and honored guest in every home, the counsellor of strong men and the children's guide?

We make much of the vantage ground offered by the city as the position where the minister of the gospel may do his largest work; and in thought perhaps we esteem lightly the country pastorate, and teach our young men to look to the apparently larger fields for influence. Here is the man, Daniel McPhail, who was content to spend his best days in Osgoode. And besides the thousands brought to Christ by his own personal ministry, he being dead yet speaketh in India wherever McLaurin for eighteen years preached the gospel in Telugu; along the Ottawa where Brierly for all too short a time told the old story; in New York where MacGregor is gathering his spiritual harvest; in Manitoba and Dakota where McDonald's pioneer work is still bearing fruit, and where McCaul's grave has scarcely grown green; in Glasgow and Liverpool where D. P. McPherson still labors; and in Ontario and Quebec wherever Walker, Dewar, and McDonald prosecuted their ministry. Scarcely another man in our ministry, Dr. Fyfe alone excepted, did the work which this man accomplished, and it was done from the vantage ground of the country pastorate. His ministry was not what to-day would be called scholarly—it partook rather of the richness of the deep things of God, which scholarly research is apt to miss or has no time for. It was true to God and wondrously kind, and stamped itself upon a whole community. Under this ministry and among the surroundings of this church Bro. McGregor took his preparatory theological training and received the impulse of heart and mind which made him what we knew

2

him to be.   He was familiar with deep theological
questions from his early youth, and well practised in
polemics.   God and the Bible were from the first his
sacred thoughts, and the Christian ministry was to
him the summit of power and responsibility.

One other thing as an element in his schooling
must not be passed by if we would accurately gauge
the forces which made up the man.   Osgoode, though
preëminently the place of the one theme and the one
book, opened its doors to thought not strictly theological, and there appeared from time to time upon the
tables and shelves of the people books of poetry, history, biography and travel, to which Bro. McGregor
had ready access, and which he read and re-read until
the entire selection was mastered—not only mastered
as to the thought, but in many cases verbally.   Many
of us know how apt he was at quotation; how he
was never at a loss for the appropriate passage of
Scripture; how he was surprisingly saved the necessity of reference, even extended selections being
furnished by his memory: and how he astonished us
by his ready familiarity with poetry.   He had de-
voured Tennyson, and, as the breath of kine is sweet
with the odor of spring grasses, so, even his spontaneous utterances were redolent of *In Memoriam*.   The
value of the few good books has often been empha-
sized.   Mr. McGregor's mental furnishing is an example of what they make possible to him who uses
them well.

Perhaps in the foregoing may be found the chief
factors of Mr. McGregor's mental and religious make-

up, and perhaps also the schools which more than any other trained him for his after work. Now comes however the period in his experience which called for complete change of plans and of life. Converted to God in his young days, the thought grew daily upon him that he must give himself to God in the special work of the ministry. In his twenty-third year this thought took definite form, and mainly through the encouragement and assistance of his twin brother it was made possible to him to plan a college course.

With the training above outlined, then, and devoid in most part of even the elementary learning of the schools, Mr. McGregor arrived at Woodstock in the autumn of the year 1870, purposing to prepare himself for the work of the Canadian Baptist ministry. Many of us can recall his appearance and demeanor at that time. His ruddy face that had got its glow in the Osgoode out of door life. Hands large and horny, that evidenced long familiarity with the axe, and a physical build that was of the sturdiest. His near friend McDiarmid used to say of him that he walked upon two young trees. But he was very modest, and very retiring. For a long time after his arrival at school he scarcely ventured an opinion. He blushed so easily, shrank into himself so painfully, and was embarrassed so constantly, that at the first he was a puzzle to not a few. This excessive discomfort however belonged only to his earlier course. It wore off gradually, and those who were inclined to think lightly of the timorous young student, if there were any, and those who were accustomed to pass him by

unnoticed, soon came to understand that beneath that
painful bashfulness and incomprehensible reserve there
dwelt a great power which was always to be respected
and which could assert itself in fine fashion if ever
trifled with.   Mr. McGregor was a master of self-depre-
ciation—the genuine thing is here meant, not the mis-
erable subterfuge which so often does duty as a pre-
face to self-appreciation.    He really was ashamed
because he was so ignorant, or because he fancied he
was.   His idea of a college, conceived upon the Osgoode farm, was an exalted creation indeed.   The
teachers were dread inapproachables and the students,
all of them, quick-witted and learned to a degree.
The place where the ministers were made was to him
holy ground, and all its inhabitants after some sort
superior beings ; and it took some time before the
process of disenchantment was complete.   Poor fellow,
what throes he suffered on account of his fancied ignorance !   He could not take part in conversation freely
for fear of this being betrayed.   And the least kindness from a senior student was regarded as a distinguished condescension.   And how he loved to praise
others and blushed if any word of praise to himself
were heard, have often been remarked by his fellow-
students.    But his throes were unnecessary bitterness
surely, for certain it is that very few even among the
seniors were as well educated as he.   His Osgoode life
had not been lived to no purpose, and very soon were
discovered in him powers far above the average endowment. His first year at Woodstock had not passed
away when students in all classes and teachers had

learned to expect great things from the modest Osgoode boy.

In his class work at Woodstock Mr. McGregor was
not noticed so much for his quickness and brilliancy
as he was for his grasp of a subject and power to retain it. He had immense capacity for plodding, and
this, together with his sound understanding, of course
resulted for him in first-class work in all departments.
His work was not as burdensome to him as he at first
supposed it would be, and it was not long before he
found he could fairly measure himself, in ability and
power to work, with the best of his fellows. It was
not in his class-room work, however, that Mr. McGregor
was specially distinguished, though in that he never
failed in reaching an honorable position. It was in
the society work and the religious and social life of
the school, and in the public life among the churches,
that he specially made his mark. Some of his best
literary work was done for the Adelphian Society of
Woodstock College. He was the essayist *par excellence;*
the president who ever gave weight and dignity to
the proceedings; the critic whose review of the evening's work was always the treat of the programme;
and at those feasts, graciously permitted by the
Faculty, when a few oysters went further and faster
than ever they did in their native element, the incomparable *postprandial* orator. How his early training
always stood him in good stead in these society affairs!
What use he made of his acquaintance with the poets,
and how reason feasted while his soul flowed during
the peregrinations of the oyster aforesaid, all old stu-

dents will remember. He was ever the life of the
company, exuberant in his wit as in his modesty.
There can be no doubt that a college man, such as he,
has the power to help or to hinder, in great measure,
both the efficiency of the college and the progress of
his fellow students. One old Brooke at Rugby was
alike efficient support to Arnold and to Brown. One
Flashman is ever a source of anxiety. Masters are
expectant of mischief, and students are either ready for
it or dreading it, and the institution thus disorganized.
Brooke should be sought out, invited, pressed into the
school, and retained there at all cost; and Flashman,
in every guise and of any parentage, should be made
go without excuse or delay. The one makes for the
benefit of all; the other is a nuisance pure and simple.
The foregoing verges on platitude certainly, if it be not
entirely across the boundary; but the truth contained
in it is not yet sufficiently recognized to be at all times
acted upon. Young McGregor's clear head and warm
heart had no small place in bringing about the wholesome atmosphere which was breathed by teachers and
students in Woodstock College during the early 70's.

But the activity of his religious life was perhaps
his most noteworthy characteristic. Conversion with
him meant much more than salvation; and religious
doctrine much more than an intellectual pastime, to
be engaged in with solemn visage. He recognized the
Christ-life as the serious business of his life, and
sought day by day in his own humble and beautiful
way to do something which would tell upon the kingdom. His hushed earnestness in prayer, as he led the

students' devotions; his quiet passion as he spoke the praises of his Redeemer in their prayer meetings; his constant and unobtrusive "personal dealing," who that knew him as a Woodstock student can fail to recall? And who did not personally, in some fashion, receive the touch of his quiet spirit, and become a better man through receiving it?

Mr. McGregor, as a student, made much of the day of rest, and always entered upon its services with quiet and holy joy. Mr. Bates and Mr. Goodspeed were his pastors in his Woodstock days; and if it may be said that few students have had more instructive pastors, it may also be said that few pastors have had a more receptive listener. Mr. McGregor revelled in the sermon, and carried with him to his room for rehearsal and the spiritual profit of others not only divisions and illustrations, but also the force and spirit of the discourse His was a wholesome college life. It developed kindred spirits and multiplied the agencies for good which at that time resulted so conspicuously in the conversion of students to God.

In his early preaching and in the spiritual work he did outside of the college he soon made it manifest to those who were intimate with his spirit and methods that he would be, and not many years in the future, a strong man in the pulpit and in denominational work. He set the pulpit before him as that to which he must make everything bend. It was the great object, so he thought, for all who were called to the work of the ministry. And he regarded it not more specially as that which demanded the best he could give, than as that which ought to compel others to yield up their best also. And in this serious business of sermonizing he was always solicitous for others as for himself. Was he not always ready to work with a tyro over his sermon plan ? Was he not generally appealed to in the matter of exegetical doubt ? And was he not ever modestly suggestive in reply to interrogations ? And so interested was he in others' work, that he has been known to tramp eight miles with a young brother who was going to that bodeful experiment—his first sermon—to encourage him, and eight miles back, to bear up his drooping spirits withal, after the initial deed was done. And his comforting was as sweet as a mother's, and his words of encouragement as well timed.

It is unnecessary to follow him through his preparatory collegiate and theological courses. These were all completed at Woodstock. His progress was easy and definite. His capacity for work and for acquisition increased with the years; as did also his mental grasp, and the power to utilize what he had attained. In the department of theology particularly his maturing powers found a congenial sphere, and here he did his best work and had his greatest joy. How well he worked, and how much he was enamoured of this department a few years were to show. He graduated in April, 1878, and his address upon "The Divine Estimate of Orthodoxy" was considered one of the most thoughtful and purposeful of the many addresses for which the platform from which he spoke was famous.

In connection with Mr. McGregor's Woodstock

career there remains to be noted that which, more than anything else, put upon him the stamp of the genuine manhood which was so apparent to all who came near to his life. Bro. McGregor's native endowments were moulded at the college by a master spirit. Dr. Fyfe was his revered preceptor of whom he used to speak as the greatest influence which ever encountered his life ; at whose feet his theological instinct was quickened and strengthened ; and in whose companionship the great graces of humility, gentleness and rugged virility were fostered to the refinement of strength. The remark is familiar, that colleges consist of men and not of facilities. Given the man of sound understanding, of true heart, simple, brave and earnest, and whether he has at his command brick and mortar, apparatus, or other much desired academic facilities or not, there will be a college at his hand in which *men* may be trained. The facilities of Woodstock College, in Bro. McGregor's time, were not remarkable—adequate however ; but there was the great collegiate force notwithstanding—a great man. Mr. McGregor fully appreciated the advantages of pursuing his theological training under Dr. Fyfe, and this appreciation continued unabated even when he himself was Professor in the same department.

In the foregoing pages nothing has been said of Bro. McGregor's faults ; this paragraph shall be devoted to one of the serious blunders of his student life.

Friend McGregor did not take kindly to the campus. He was innocent of athletics in any form, if he had not indeed a decided distaste for anything of the kind. When he arrived at Woodstock, as has been said, he was fresh from the farm, broad-chested, sturdy-legged, and muscular, as few young men are. His occupation hitherto had given him an out of door life, and constant play to his superb physique. He was unwise, as many young men are, in fancying he could let go any special care of the body. His exercise was limited to the sidewalk between the college and the town, with the unfailing result, physical collapse—at least partially so—necessitating a year's absence from his studies for purposes of recuperation. This, however, affected less or more his bodily comfort ever afterward. Not that he became valetudinarian by any means, but that the stamina, the powers of endurance which he once possessed so abundantly had left him forever; and doubtless in some measure this blunder of his life had not a little to do with the sad untimeliness of his end.

It is to be supposed that Mr. McGregor planned for himself a thorough collegiate course, and a theological course, and then liberty to enter upon his much loved work. This was the extent of preparation commonly received by ministerial students at that time; and had he, when he formed his plans, had anything more extensive in mind, he would hardly have pursued his theological before his arts course. It is presumed that he discovered what so many others have also discovered, that for the ministry of Jesus Christ every preparation possible is demanded. And sadly feeling his further need, even after he had completed his Woodstock studies he resolved upon University work. The carrying out of such a resolution required persistent grace and pluck. Mr. McGregor had no funds, and but few friends of the funded sort on whom he might rely for assistance. It meant for him that he must go through a scheme of work requiring the full time of the average man, and at the same time he must earn his bread. He was not daunted, however, but bravely faced what he knew the years following would bring to him. He entered the second year of University work, taking the honor course in metaphysics, and with it some required subjects of the first year. One looking back at the curriculum of '78 will see that to compass satisfactorily the work there laid down as above indicated, would not give to the best of men many spare days during the year. But Mr. McGregor must take, in connection with it, the pastoral charge of two churches. It will easily be seen that he was thus greatly handicapped. He went personally every second week to Whitby and Brooklin, and frequently on the alternating Sunday, from inability to secure a supply, leaving Toronto on Friday generally, and returning Monday. His Sabbath work consisted of three preaching services and a drive of between seven and eight miles. Occasionally the pastoral work was so pressing that much more extended draughts upon his time were made necessary. At one time he did not begin his University work until after Christmas. From his conception of the Christian ministry it could not be otherwise than that he should give to his church work good and honest service, whatever might come of his studies, and that he gave such work those who enjoyed his ministry in '78 and '79 can give glad testimony. God blessed him abundantly, and many were added to the churches. On Monday mornings he would return to the city exhausted, and not until the following day was he in any fit state to begin his work.

At the beginning of his last year in the University he resigned the charge of the churches, that he might have less care and more time to devote his energies to the final struggle; but he found it necessary to supply surrounding churches as vacancies occurred, and finally he arrived at the end of his course, having made a hard fight of it but finishing triumphant. He was lauriated in Convocation Hall in May, 1881, together with J. H. Doolittle, P. K. Dayfoot, D. Grant, and J. J. Baker, kindred spirits with whom he had read and prayed and preached during many a year of student labor. In a letter to a friend he makes playful allusion to the final scene of his student life. "Here am I sitting alone in the night looking to that piece of parchment or pelt, seeking in vain for some transmogrifying influence which, alas, never comes. If that parchment be genuine sheepskin then I perceive the wisdom of the Senate of the University in choosing such significant material upon which to inscribe degrees. In all likelihood they have also chosen, or had suggested to them, the title of B.A. from the expiring cry of the original owner of the wondrous pelt." So ended the years of technical study—through them all he had done well, and he entered upon his Stratford pastorate a strong man well furnished.

Some few characteristics of his University life will be in place before bringing this chapter to a close. In his mental make-up Bro. McGregor was nothing if not logical ; yet in his habits of study strange to say he was the most illogical of men. Restlessly nervous, he would become fevered in his anxiety to accomplish his task, and would read furiously very frequently all the night long. So conscientious was he that the prescribed reading must be done at any cost, and it was done often at the expense of that which ought to have been carefully guarded. Only an unusual physical vigor could stand the strain, and he did not go unscathed.

The incessant toil of over pressing study is never in itself conducive to pronounced spirituality. There are very few students who have not to confess a sad decadence of zeal and a manifest waning of the glow and force of the religious impulse during a protracted term of study. Not even do they escape whose attention is devoted almost exclusively to the study of sacred things. Divinity students as well as others must be on guard lest the light within them become darkness. Our brother was an exception to this too common rule. Through the long period of his devotion to special studies his spiritual powers suffered no eclipse. Indeed it is had upon very good testimony, that in all that characterized his religious life he grew daily and manifestly towards the ideal. His faithfulness to God's word, and his love for it, never weakened through these years ; and those intimate with his life knew him to be ever increasingly a lover of Jesus Christ. He had passed the period of doubt and

of questioning earlier than most men, and upon his
graduation his feet were upon the rock, to abide there
ever more.   In this experience he owed much to his
early training, and surely he went to his work better
conditioned in every way than the graduate who has
still before him the encounter with the unrest of
doubt.  Not that everything was clear to his spiritual
vision, by any means, and not that he had not his share
of perplexity ; but his faith had deepened wondrously,
and was unmovably rooted upon the Eternal ; so that
he had but one answer to his own or to another's in-
terrogation upon all matters affecting providence or
faith—" The day will declare it."   Strong in this conclusion which he had found in the subsoil of Christian
thought, he was contented to go on every day with
his day's work and have faith in God.

And here another thing should be said of him.  He
sat at the feet of Dr. Young throughout his University career, and came through that ordeal with the
Christian life broadened and deepened, certainly with
no mark of any philosophy upon him that would remove his thought from God.   This statement is made
because something more tangible than hint has been
floating through air reflecting upon the tendency of
the late Dr. Young's philosophical teaching.   Bro.
McGregor benefited vastly under his instruction, and
was accustomed to speak of him in terms indicating
his reverence for the man and his appreciation of the
inspiration of his instruction.

This chapter must now close, and as the last words
are being penned there comes to the writer the mem-

ory of him who has left us just as he was when he
stepped from the restraints of college into the full
activities and responsibilities of manhood life. Student
habits, and years of absence from the conditions of his
earlier life, had left their impression upon him physi-
cally. The ruddy face had gone, and the horny hand.
Mingled with the lines of uncommon strength of character, which were always manifest, there were the indications of sweetness and gentleness. Of stout
physical build still, yet he lacked the sturdiness of his
early manhood—flesh as abundant, but not muscular
as of yore. Through the blunder referred to elsewhere he had allowed his clay, even while it was re-
fined perhaps, to deteriorate. Strong mentally even
at the first, he now had developed unusual mental
vigor, and was admitted *facile princeps* by all who
worked with him. He was no longer as we first
knew him, the retiring, blushing, self-depreciative
student ; but one who had become aggressive and as-
sertive, one who knew his powers and had trained
them for use, and did use them, always kindly and
gently, but with tremendous force, as we all know
when right was to be maintained, or any righteous
cause to be championed. As the Christian man however, first and last, he was distinguished. He entered
school filled with the simplicity of the gospel of Jesus:
he graduated, if such a thing could be, a still more
simple-minded and humble man. He had gotten
wisdom and understanding, but characterizing him
through and through, in thought, word, and deed, was
the fear of the Lord his first and last acquisition.

# CHAPTER III.

## THE PASTORATE.

A.D. 1878-'86.

In attempting to write on the pastoral work of our lamented brother, any one who has not been his constant companion in labor must feel himself unequal to the undertaking. The difficulty is greatly increased by the excessive modesty which characterized his life. The one who, above all others, knew his life and work writes : " Mr. McGregor worked so quietly and had such a humble estimate of himself and his work that it is difficult to fix upon items of special interest. Even with myself, although the tenderest confidence existed between us, he would refer half-shrinkingly to interesting matters in his work as if fearful that it might seem like self-praise."

Another, from whom information has been sought, writes : " He was such a reticent man that after a whole day's visiting amongst his people he rarely uttered a word about his experiences;" and the testimony of a third is, that " his modesty made him slow to feel that what related to himself would be of interest to others." These are qualities which, excellent in themselves, compel the biographer to leave the record much more barren than the life has been.   Notwithstanding this difficulty, enough can be written to show that our brother possessed, in an unusual degree, the elements of a true leader of God's hosts in each and every phase of an office vested in one person by the Great Head of the church, and termed bishop, elder, presbyter and pastor—not different offices, as some think, but different appellations designating the several phases of the one heaven-appointed office, each significantly setting forth a part of the leader's work, and all combined presenting the sacred calling in its many-sided character.

The qualities of mind and heart necessary to the fulfilment of an office requiring such diversity of gifts were, in an extraordinary degree, the endowment of pastor McGregor. As *bishop* (in the Gospel conception of that term), how he labored to take heed unto himself and to all the flock over which the Holy Spirit had made him bishop (R.V.), to feed the church of God, which He purchased with His own blood ! He spared neither time nor effort to prepare himself to give unto the flock "the sincere milk" and "strong meat" of the word of life. Publicly and from house to house his ministry was such as to stimulate and encourage the faintest desires after the better life, and feed the most advanced Christian with wholesome diet. As *presbyter* or *elder*, he manifested the true gravity and dignity pertaining to his sacred calling. As *pastor*, he proved himself a true shepherd, ever careful to imitate the life of Him who is, in the highest sense, "the Shepherd and Bishop of our souls."

The pastoral work of our beloved brother com-

3

menced with the churches in Whitby and Brooklin, on the 28th day of April, 1878—less than one year after his graduation from Woodstock College. In Whitby he was publicly ordained to the ministry on the sixth day of the following June. In this field he labored in the Gospel until October, 1880. During this pastorate the amount of work done by him was simply prodigious. He preached three times every Lord's day, did a large amount of other pastoral work, and, at the same time, prosecuted his studies at the University of Toronto; and *every part* of his work was thoroughly done. His fidelity to his work as a student, and his mastery of the subjects of the course pursued are not within the province of this chapter. We are glad to be able to say that the faithful attention to his studies that gained for him the respectable standing that was his, was never allowed to interfere with the best possible preparation for his pulpit work. So much was this the case, that his successor in the field of his first pastorate writes: "By many of the people here he is still looked upon as the 'Prince of Preachers,' while as a pastor he endeared himself to every one with whom he came in contact." Nor did his class and pulpit preparation absorb all his time and thought. In his note-book we find a detailed account of the Christian experience and baptism of sixteen persons during his short pastorate at Whitby and Brooklin. Few persons appreciated the power of the pulpit and the need of preparation for meeting its exalted claims more than he; yet he regarded the pastoral visitation which gave opportunities for personal contact with souls, resulting in gathering into the church of God "hand-picked fruit," as not one whit less important, and perhaps even more important, than the pulpit, and for this department of the pastoral office he showed rare tact and ability. In his note-book are to be found the following wise suggestions which grew out of his own experience:

"Would it not be well in pastoral work, especially among members of the church, to get from them the time of their conversion, the ground of their hope, and their Christian experience, difficulties and joys, etc., noting this down for future reference? This would keep in memory what it is well for pastors to know, and what we otherwise should forget. It would help us to help them, and would be a source of profit to us in comparing the experiences of Christians, in helping those in doubt, and in discerning the working of the Spirit in the hearts of the unconverted." So thoroughly was he acquainted with the experiences of his church members, and so rare were his skill and tact in dealing with the anxious and unconverted, that he must have carried these suggestions into practice in his own work.

The success of his pastorate in Whitby is not to be measured by the number added to the church roll during his term of service, nor was the influence of his life confined to the church to which he directly ministered. The present pastor of these churches writes, that "more than one, who are now members of other churches in this town, remember him as the instrumental cause of their conversion. His influence was widely felt outside of his own congregation, and

I often hear him spoken of as a man of great piety and singular winsomeness."

His resignation of the charge of these churches in October, 1880, was caused solely by the conviction that the closing studies of his University course must have his undivided attention. "His resignation here," writes one that knows, "was received with profound regret, while the great work he was afterwards permitted to do in Stratford and Toronto was a source of great rejoicing to the friends he left upon this field." In January, 1881, a call came from the church in Stratford, Ontario. After some hesitation, caused by want of acquaintance with the field, the call was accepted, on condition that he be permitted to complete his course of studies in Toronto University before entering upon his work.

Shortly after accepting the call to Stratford, Mr. McGregor received a letter from the Secretary of the American Baptist Missionary Union, urging him to accept an appointment to Japan, to superintend the work of Bible translation. Coming just as he was completing his University work, this call occasioned considerable wavering in reference to his plans for future work. But having already given his promise to Stratford he felt constrained to abide by that decision ; the more so perhaps as his thoughts had been drawn towards India as the most desirable field for missionary labor. During all his college course there was a secret longing for and looking to India, and had the way been open when he finished his course, to India no doubt he would have gone.

He writes to a friend concerning the beginning of his work in Stratford, in the following words: "I wrote my last examination on the morning of May the 23rd, and the evening of that day found me walking the streets of Stratford. My first pastoral duty was the uniting in Hymen's bonds of two young lives who had decided to continue the voyage of life in one canoe." Auspicious beginning of five and one-half of, perhaps, the happiest years of his bright and happy life. On reaching the field he writes: "The cause here is neither large nor strong. I think, however, that there are in the church the elements of power, and that the field is one where labor will not be in vain. I think I shall like much to labor in Stratford." With intense interest and Christlike consecration he took up his work here, preaching publicly and privately. Three weeks after he entered upon his work he writes: "I have visited over fifty families and have not yet covered the field," *Fifty families* in three weeks! How does that compare with the work of the ordinary pastor? Yet he never appeared before his people on Lord's day with unbeaten oil; nor were his pastoral visits formal calls with no higher motive than to keep on popular terms with his congregation.

Pastor McGregor went to his pastorate prepared to love the flock over which the Holy Spirit made him overseer, with the same kind of love which the Great Shepherd Himself, whom he constantly sought to imitate, manifested. Because he loved them he yearned to be helpful to them; in order to help them he must know them; and to know them he must be among

them, in their homes and at their work, when their
work would not be hindered by his presence.

One of his Stratford members gave me recently the
following incident, which deserves to be recorded as
a tribute to his memory; it also serves to bring out
one of the essential characteristics of the true pastor.
The good brother, being a farmer, suffered severely
from a terrific hail-storm that destroyed all his crop.
The church on hearing of his loss collected quite a
sum of money for the impoverished brother, the pastor taking an active part in the work.  He drove ten
miles to visit his parishioner with the gift, and found
him downcast and discouraged.  After a few words
of sympathy and cheer he threw off his coat, and
with the sunshine of his presence and the assistance
of his arm he spent the day with that brother in the
field, driving away his despondency and turning his
sorrow into joy.  When seated in his carriage to
leave, he placed in the hand of him whose heart was
already overflowing with gratitude a roll of bank bills,
which scattered the few clouds that yet remained on
his financial sky.  Next year, instead of the hail-
stone, came the sunshine and the gentle shower upon
this brother's crop, and at the next annual meeting of
the church, with gratitude to his brethren, especially
to his pastor, he placed the amount of money at the
disposal of the church.  This body magnanimously
bestowed the amount upon the pastor, and thus the
bread cast upon the waters returned after many days.

The joy of his people was his joy, and if sorrow
or reverses darkened the home of any of them the

shadow crossed his threshold also. Even in his last illness, when news came concerning two Stratford homes that had been visited with sore trial, he had brokenness of spirit to an alarming degree. For many days he mingled prayer and tears in behalf of the troubled ones. Again his heart was filled with joy just as intense as the preceding sorrow, when word come to him as he lay suffering in St. Luke's Hospital, New York, that Stratford was enjoying a season of revival. From the very beginning of his ministry in Stratford he stole the hearts of the people, not with the deceitful methods of a designing Absalom, but with the magnetism of a life surcharged with the spirit of Jesus the Christ. I cannot conceive it possible for any man to be more deeply entrenched in the affections of any people than is the lamented D. A. McGregor, even to-day, in the affections of the people of Stratford.

Here, permit one of his honored deacons to speak : "As a minister he was on the most cordial terms with ministers of other denominations, and in meetings of a union nature he took his place amongst them with a grace and modest dignity peculiarly his own. His preaching was characterized by intense earnestness, profound reasoning and a clear logical presentation of the truth. He relied upon no trick of the would-be orator for effect, but on the living truth of God, which he so faithfully proclaimed. With earnest words and grave he reasoned of rightousness, temperance and judgment to come, and with deep pathos and winning tenderness he besought men to be reconciled to God; while the doctrines of our holy religion and the distinguishing tenets of the denomination he loved so dearly and served so well found in him an earnest champion and a valiant and successful defender. But high as he ranked as a preacher, it was perhaps as a pastor that he even more excelled. He was at once the wise and judicious counsellor and the faithful and sympathetic friend. The weak and the erring were encouraged and reproved by him with rare tact and discrimination. He had the happy faculty of winning the esteem, love and confidence of his flock to an unusual degree; so much so, that he was looked upon by all as a dear personal friend. In social life, the sparkle and glow of his ready wit and delicate humor made him a most agreeable companion; yet he never forgot that true dignity which so well becomes the Christian minister, and the unfailing result of intercourse with him was to be lifted into a higher plane. With the duties of the Secretaryship of the Home Mission Board and the cares of the pastorate, his was a busy life; yet he was never too busy to respond to the call of duty, or so engrossed with his own cares as to be unmindful of the cares of others. He was the very embodiment of constancy and loyalty to what he believed to be duty."

His ministry in Stratford from its very commencement was one of power and blessing. Perpetual manifestations of God's smile were the lot of pastor and people. In addition to his regular work, he organized a weekly meeting with the young men of his church, for the purpose of assisting them in Bible study, of helping them in their spiritual difficulties, and of developing the desire and ability to attempt and pursue Christian work. He was an ardent lover of the young. They had in him a tender-hearted sympathizer and a true friend. Whenever he met a young man who gave any promise of power, he coveted him for the gospel ministry.

He also conducted a normal class, comprising the entire church membership, for the study of Bible doctrine. Through his whole pastorate he urged upon his people the necessity of being able to give to every one that asked them a reason for their hope and belief, and he spared no pains to assist them so to do. He believed that no man should be a Baptist simply because he happened to have been cradled in a Baptist home, but rather that every one should have a "thus saith the Lord" for his faith and practice; and he was determined, so far as *his* people were concerned, that they should know what they believed and why they believed it. The "sword of the spirit" was a tried weapon in his own hand, and with remarkable skill and power he wielded it. He labored that the membership of his church also should be acquainted with the word and should know how to use it.

His views of God's word were remarkably clear, and his grasp of truth was that of a giant. His ability to deal with men in every shade of spiritual difficulty was marvelous. No honest inquirer could have an interview with him without being benefited. Power and tenderness were peculiarly blended in his nature.

Every one that entered into conversation with him was at once captivated by the wonderful combination of his unique character.    While he gave special attention to the building of Christian character in those who were within the fold, he by no means neglected those that were without.    Like his blessed Master, his heart yearned over lost souls.    He believed the teachings of God's word in regard to eternal punishment awaiting the finally impenitent, as well as in relation to the blessed immortality of the saved.    He shuddered at the doom of the wicked, and sought with intense earnestness to pluck them as brands from the burning.    He was naturally of a buoyant spirit and rarely depressed, but on these rare occasions the cause almost invariably found expression in words like these: "What a burden it would lift from life could we

> "But trust that good will fall
> At last—far off—at last to all."

But he never could find any scriptural ground for such trust, though he sought it diligently.    He read widely in reference to "the larger hope," bringing the utterances of men under the touchstone of God's word, and having gone over the ground thoroughly he remarked, "I find nothing in revealed truth to favor 'the larger hope.'"

He had unbounded faith in the Gospel of Jesus Christ as the power of God unto the salvation of souls, and he often expressed surprise that men would not accept its provisions and secure its gifts.    His feelings in this regard are couched in Faber's beautiful lines :

" Souls of men why will ye scatter
Like a crowd of frightened sheep ?
Foolish hearts ! why will ye wander
From a love so true and deep ? "

He was restless to present the gospel to needy souls
on every possible occasion. Not only was he a lover
of souls, it pleased God to make him essentially a
winner of souls. This was the business of his life.
Wooing men by his love, convincing them by his
logic, it was his joy to see many submit themselves to
Christ. In his note-book he writes : " Must we wait
for an introduction before speaking to a person about
his soul ? Must the watchman be introduced to a citi-
zen before he can tell him that his house is on fire?"
Upon this principle he ever acted. He waited not
for an introduction, but in the market, in shop or
store, in the banker's office or in the livery stable,
wherever there was a soul he saw an opportunity for
presenting the gospel and he took advantage of it.
Bright and cheerful though he was, there was, nevertheless, in his manner and conversation a pleasing
seriousness that caused one to expect him to talk of
Christ and His gospel, and that made it easy for him
to turn any conversation into serious channels. It was
interesting to watch with what delicacy and tact he
would approach people in regard to their souls' interest. Barriers of pride, haughtiness and sullenness
gave way at once, and stern business men and ultra-
fashionable women, not a few, have been known to
put away all reserve, and converse freely with him of
doubts and hopes and felt needs.

In conversation on difficulty in reaching men, he

was once asked if he ever met with a rebuff. "Why no," he replied, "I don't think I ever have," and it seemed to dawn upon him for the first time that it was strange that he had not. People trusted him instinctively and were led, almost unconsciously, to reveal to him on slightest acquaintance thoughts and aspirations that are carefully guarded, in many cases, even from those of one's own household. Two examples of this spontaneous confidence may be given. Passing hurriedly along the street one morning this soul-lover overtook an old man whom he had seen in church a short time before. He shook hands with the old gentleman, asking about his health. Appealingly, tremuously the answer came—" Mr. McGregor, I wish it were as well with my soul as it is with my body." Briefly and tenderly the way of life was set before this troubled one. Passers by guessed not the import of the earnest words exchanged by those two men on the public highway that morning, but a soul entered into peace. Two or three years afterwards word came. " Old Mr. R. passed away triumphantly saying, ' I am going home.'"

Another day, on his way to the post-office, he met an Indian evidently in great distress of mind. Before he had time to speak the poor alarmed fellow said to him, "Can you forgive my sins, sir ?" " No," was the reply, "only God can forgive sins," and he quoted several passages in relation to forgiveness. " Well," said the excited man, " that must be true, I know it is true (this Indian was intelligent, and had some knowledge of the Bible), but I have just come from

the priest, and he told me that he alone could forgive
my sins and I would have to pay ten dollars. I hadn't
that much money and he said I must go to hell then,
and I am so afraid of the big fire." Drawing a silver
rosary out of his pocket he threw it into the street,
saying, " I'll never confess to the priest again." His
new spiritual adviser told him, if he was sincere in
his determination to seek forgiveness, he would like
to retain the rosary as a pledge of his sincerity. The
Indian, now quiet and composed, said he meant what
he promised. After some searching they found the
rosary in the dust, and Mr. McGregor preserved it in
memory of this trophy of Divine grace. He never
heard of his new friend after this; but he often spoke
of him and wondered if in " that day " he will be
found among the number who shall have escaped the
" big fire." He was instant in season and out of season.
The writer has vivid recollections of him a few weeks
before his last illness as he stood on a railway platform, awaiting the coming train, and with a counte-
nance aglow with earnestness and eyes moist with soul
emotion he sought to direct an anxious soul into the
way of salvation. The soul struggling towards the
light was sure to be assisted in his company. His
own hope had but a feeble beginning, and the memory
of that fact made him very careful lest his words to
the anxious should have a tendency to " break the
bruised reed or quench the smoking flax." "I seemed,"
he said, referring to his own conversion, " to have
grasped a thread only and all the way home I feared
lest it should break ; but it held." He also knew in

common with other true Christians what doubts were.
In an old letter he writes, "I can understand the
blinding power of feeling, how it can make the most
living experience of life appear unreal.   Therefore I
cannot wonder that doubts should sometimes rise with
bewildering power, causing one to be suspicious of the
reality of the most incontestable experiences of life."
He often said that he would be very fearful for the
life that had never known a doubt, saying

> " There is no shadow
> Where there is no sun."

He prized John's Epistles and recommended them to
the fearful.   "There is," said he, "so much to encourage and assure in the oft reiterated ' we know.' "

Faithful and mighty as a preacher, and effective as
a winner of souls, he was also wise and considerate as
a disciplinarian.   In dealing with difficulties between
members of the church he never permitted any feeling of sensitiveness or delicacy on his own part to
prevent the carrying out of our Lord's instructions in
Matthew xviii : 15-17.   If any were unwilling to take
these steps he regarded it as conclusive evidence that
spiritual life was at a very low ebb.   Naturally he
was very sensitive, but in every thing that pertained
to the welfare of the church he lost sight of self entirely.   He did not look for offences, and they rarely
came.   Did he give offence himself, he lost no time in
seeking an interview and offering apology if he were
in fault.   Nor did he feel that this course of conduct
belittled his calling or detracted from his proper per-

sonal dignity. Writing to a friend in reference to church matters he says: "I think there would be fewer difficulties between pastor and people if we, as pastors, so lived as to impress our people with this thought, that we are constantly about our Master's business."

As he brought power to the pulpit and wisdom to the counsels of his brethren, so he brought sunshine and consolation into the home of the sick and the otherwise afflicted. Among those who were blessed with his cheerful and helpful visits on such occasions his memory is very fragrant.

During his pastorate in Stratford the war against intemperance waged hotly, and this hater of all evil threw himself into the fight with great enthusiasm. He had watched the results of intoxicating liquors in the lives of men until his heart grew sick. It was a rule in his home, that no beggar or "tramp" should be turned hungry from his door. While the physical wants were being supplied he busied himself in finding the cause of their impoverished or homeless condition, never failing to direct them to Him who, "though he was rich yet for our sakes became poor, that we through his poverty might be made rich," and who prepared a home for the wanderer and opened wide its door. Almost without exception every such case, and they were very many, he found to be the product of drink. He opposed the evil on every possible occasion, by precept and example, and one of the most humiliating things to him in his last illness was to be compelled to take brandy as a stimulant. "Oh

how I hate the stuff!" he would exclaim, and he did
hate it both for what it is in itself and for what it is
doing.

During his work in the College it gave him great
joy to be permitted to return to either of the fields on
which he had labored, the only trouble being the difficulty of parting again with the people, many of whom
were his spiritual children and as dear to him as his
own life. A few days before his death, speaking of
the prospect of returning to his work in the autumn
(as the physicians hoped), he remarked: "If it were
merely a question of personal pleasure the pastorate
would be more inviting"; but he felt that the College
work presented a broader field of usefulness. Once
again, while in the hospital, he spoke of the pastorate
with *great tenderness*. It seemed to give him peculiar pleasure to take a backward glance at the years
thus spent; not because he gloried in the work done,
but because he rejoiced in having been allowed the
privilege of doing it. As to his estimate of his own
work he wrote: "In some few things I think my
heart does not condemn me, but I should rejoice
in recovery if so be that I might redeem the time.
Still I have decided not to mourn always over past
failures, but to strive to find rest and comfort in the
truth that salvation is all of grace and not at all of
works."

Notwithstanding his wonderful adaptability to
every department of the pastor's work, it ought to be
recorded for the benefit of others, that during the
first year of his pastorate a natural timidity, increased

by a clear apprehension of awful responsibility, gave him more than a little trouble. He often walked to and fro for some minutes in front of the house he was about to visit, seeking to overcome the natural shrinking from meeting and conversing with the inmates; but he struggled against this feeling until family visitation became to him, perhaps, the most delightful and to his people the most helpful department of the many-sided office. He loved the pastorate and in all its departments he magnified his office. With adoring gratitude he thanked Christ Jesus the Lord that he counted him faithful, appointing him to His service. A keen sense of his own unworthiness was ever present with him, but the fullest appreciation of the worthiness of Jesus Christ and his true relation to Him was a large factor in making him the humble, faithful, and successful pastor that he was. "He is the best man," says Dr. Stuart—"the fullest of God and of human brotherhood—in whose heart is deepest written, 'Worthy is the Lamb that was slain.'" No one could be long in Mr. McGregor's company without feeling that this precious truth was deeply written on his heart, and that its impress found expression in the actions of his consecrated life. Among his papers are to be found four sermons, and more than twice that number of partly prepared plans of sermons, on this soul-touching text—"Worthy is the Lamb that was slain."

The sentiment here expressed will be confirmed by the following extract from a letter received a few weeks ago from the beloved and sorely bereaved

4

partner of his youth, and sharer of his joys and sorrows : "I went into his room one day and found him deeply absorbed in thought.  He said, 'I am working over that text, 'Worthy is the Lamb.'  How wonderful it is!'  Going into the study on another occasion to put his papers in order, I picked up a scrap written over with the words 'dear Jesus,' 'dear Jesus,' oft repeated. I scanned them with tender reverence, for well I knew that the pen had unconsciously written the sentiment of the writer's heart as he studied and exulted in the matchless beauty of the person and character of Christ."

Seven months after Mr. McGregor settled down to hard work in Stratford a fresh impetus was given to the work by his marriage, on the 28th day of December, 1881, to Miss Augusta J. Hull, eldest daughter of James H. Hull, Esq., of Princeton, Ontario. This new home set up in the midst of his people had in it all the elements of an ideal home, and from it emanated influences that are not yet lost upon the homes of the congregation.  The already happy home was made happier by the advent, on the 28th of September, 1882, of their first-born daughter, Edith Louise.  In all, five children were born into the family, two in Stratford and three in Toronto : Gertrude Clementina on May 13th, 1884 ; Arthur Robert on July 8th, 1886 ; Enid (who died the day of her birth), July 2nd, 1888 ; and Enid Augusta, June 14th, 1889. On September 7th, 1888, only two months and five days after the death of the first Enid, the parents were called upon to suffer a calamity and a shock of extraordinary severity. Their bright, their beautiful, their promising and only boy, Arthur, the delight and hope of their hearts, was suddenly snatched from their embrace by that fell disease diphtheria. That wound was never healed. Under it Mr. McGregor almost succumbed; and such was the prolonged pain of it that, to his dying day, he scarcely ever could trust himself to speak of it to any one.

Reference has been made to the increase of joy that came into the home when Edith Louise was born, but pen cannot record the ecstasy with which the afflicted father, prostrated in a New York hospital, received the tidings that Edith Louise was, in her eighth year, *born again.* A short time before his departure he wrote to his wife the following beautiful sentences concerning the loved ones who passed through their happy home to the happier one over yonder: "I often think of our little ones who are in the upper fold. Some day, O some day we shall see them, and know them, and they shall not be ignorant of us. They and we shall rejoice together, and our joy no one will take from us." This joy is now his. Reader, will you join them and share the joy which is unspeakable and full of glory?

Although the pastorate of the Stratford church was ample to fill the mind and tax the energies of any man who could content himself with an ordinary share of service, he by no means confined his work to Stratford. The village of Sebringville was one of the places that shared in his extra labors. As he was sitting in his study one day in the spring of

1884, an elderly gentleman called to say that the little German church in the village of S. was becoming so weak that they found it very difficult to sustain the ministry of the word, and that many of the young people were anxious for English preaching. The purpose of his visit was to see if it were possible for Mr. McGregor to visit them occasionally. In this request he promptly and cheerfully acquiesced, visiting the village frequently during the summer; and in November of that same year, assisted by members of his own church, he held a series of special meetings, which resulted in a very gracious and genuine awakening. On December 14th, 1884, *fourteen* happy converts were baptized as a partial result of this work, and the little struggling cause received an impetus which has continued unto this day. His own work at home was never allowed to flag. Constant evidences of the divine approval were his joy; but the most remarkable ingathering of souls followed the special work at Sebringville, thus proving that in more ways than one there is that scattereth and yet increaseth.

Added to his manifold duties as pastor and missionary was the work of preparing the notes on the Sunday School lessons for the *Canadian Baptist*, which work he prosecuted to the satisfaction and profit of all his readers; and yet again his brethren, evidently recognizing the fact that his many and brilliant talents were accumulating by their constant use, pressed upon him, in April, 1884, an appointment to the Home Mission secretaryship for Ontario. His

make-up was such that he found it exceedingly difficult to refuse to bear any burden tending to advance
the interest of the Redeemer's kingdom. On this new
field he saw a great work to be done and he bent all
the reserved energy of his many-sided life to its
accomplishment. This appointment was no mere sine-
cure. The labor and anxiety entailed by it were suffi-
cient to tax the energies of an ordinary man with
nothing else to attend to, and the work he did in connection with this appointment was simply enormous.
All his former work in the pastorate he continued,
with the exception of his Young Men's Bible-class
which he was compelled, very reluctantly, to abandon.

The more familiar he became with the state of the
mission fields, the stronger grew the conviction that a
secretary who was at the same time a pastor could not
do justice to this work. "We need," he said, "a
strong, earnest man to give his whole time and attention to the development of our Home Mission work,
opening up new fields, strengthening weak causes, etc."
He used every possible effort to bring this about, and
when, in the autumn of 1884, Rev. Alexander Grant
was appointed General Superintendent of Home Missions, no one rejoiced more than he. The appointment
of Mr. Grant may not have lightened the work of the
Secretary very materially, for the correspondence
steadily increased, but he felt that there was at least
a sharing of the responsibility.

As in the pastorate he endeared himself to every
member of his church, so in the secretaryship of Missions he endeared himself to every missionary on the

field.  The hard-working, poorly-paid, oft-discouraged
missionary found in the secretary a true sympathizer
—an invaluable friend and helper.  The onerous duties
of this office he performed with marvellous skill and
ability.    Should any misunderstanding arise between
the Board and one of its missionaries, the presence of
this man would prove as oil upon the troubled waters,
or even a letter from his facile pen would turn the
storm into a calm.  In viewing the proud position held
by the Home Mission work of the denomination to-
day, the name of Daniel Arthur McGregor must be
remembered as a powerful factor in attaining to it.

In the year 1885 Mr. Timpany, of precious memory,
died, and the call came forth for some one to fill the
gap in our ranks in India.    Some time passed with
no response, and Mr. McGregor felt the pressure to
such a degree that in complete self-abandonment he
gave himself up to God's disposal with India in view.
He pleaded with the Lord for direction.   The conviction grew upon him that he should offer himself to
the Foreign Mission Board.   He laid the matter before his brethren, and though but a short time before
they warmly resented the approaches of another
church that had called him, they now showed a willingness to release him, though with sad hearts. Having written to his brother in reference to the care of
his little girls, he went to Woodstock to offer himself
to the Board.    While there some subtle influences
arising from circumstances outside his control changed
his purpose entirely.   The desire to go to India was
completely removed and he returned to his home and

his charge with mind at rest. He felt impelled to re-trace his steps, and subsequent events confirmed him in the assurance that he did right. His people in Stratford gladly welcomed him back, knowing how unflinchingly he ever moved in the pathway of duty as it was made plain to him. They rightly judged that these rapid changes in his plans were not the outcome of a vacillating mind, but that God was prov-ing His servant.

Notwithstanding the large amount of time and thought that he gave to the work of the kingdom outside the limits of his own pastorate, his work at home was never neglected and the blessing of success was never withheld. During the five and one-half years of his ministry in Stratford, it was his privilege to receive into the fellowship of the church by bap-tism one hundred and twenty-one persons, and by letter and experience sixty-two. "He was repeatedly approached by other churches offering larger material support," writes one of his honored deacons, "but believing his work here not yet completed to all of them he turned a deaf ear, and amply did he feel repaid in the rich blessing that attended his ministry. But when, on the 9th day of June, 1886, the appoint-ment to a professorship in Toronto Baptist College was with such unanimity pressed upon his acceptance, he resigned his pastorate. The church recognizing in him a peculiar fitness for the work to which he had been called released him from his charge by passing unanimously the following resolution: " Whereas, our beloved pastor, Rev. D. A. McGregor, B.A., has tendered his resignation of the pastorate of this church to accept a professorship in the Toronto Baptist College, Resolved, that we accept the same, recognizing as we do in him an eminent fitness for the performance of the duties of the responsible position to which in the providence of God he has been called.

"But while we accept his resignation, we cannot but give expression to our feelings of deep regret at the severance of the tie that has bound together pastor and people in the Master's service for the last five years, notwithstanding that efforts have been made to woo and win him from us by those in a position to offer higher pecuniary inducements. Gratefully we review the frequent tokens of Divine approval which have marked the union, and we trust that in our memories will ever linger fragrant recollections of a life that has been amongst us a constant proof of the truth and power of those principles which he has so faithfully proclaimed; and we can assure him that our earnest prayers will follow him to his new field of labor; and our hope and trust is, that God's richest blessings may be abundantly bestowed upon him, his partner in life and his family in the home to which they go."

His future career was watched with much interest by his Stratford friends, and when the principalship of the College was conferred upon him none were more sincere in their congratulations than they. During his long and wasting illness "prayer was made earnestly of the church unto God for him," that, if in accordance with God's will, his valuable life might be spared to his family, to the denomination, and to the work to which he had been called ; and, if not, that like gold purified by fire he might through suffering be fitted for nobler service in the higher sphere. And when the sad news of his death came with all its crushing force, even then, in that sad hour, we could look up through our tears and thank God for such a life, and that more than five years of it were lived amongst us. Truly " the memory of the just is blessed."

At a special meeting of the church it was unanimously resolved that pastor Macdonald and deacon Sharman represent the church at his funeral in Toronto. But such was the sympathy manifested, that six others volunteered to accompany them to take one more look at the face they loved so well and to follow his remains to their last resting place.

He rests from his labors, but his works follow him.

# CHAPTER IV.

## PROFESSOR AND PRINCIPAL.

### A. D. 1886-'90.

For some years before Mr. McGregor's appointment to a professorship in Toronto Baptist College there had been a growing conviction among those best acquainted with his intellectual and spiritual capabilities and attainments, that he could most efficiently serve the denomination and the cause of Christ in the professoriate of the College. It will interest readers of this memoir to know that long before Dr. Fyfe, who beyond most men knew what was in the men with whom he came into close contact, had marked Mr. McGregor as one whom the Lord would use in carrying forward the educational work to which he himself had given the best years of his life. An honored minister, who served as theological examiner at the Institute the year of Mr. McGregor's graduation from the Theological Department, has kindly furnished us with some reminiscences of the final examination in Systematic Theology: "I have a most vivid recollection," he writes, "of that examination. The room was crowded with visitors and a large number of

pastors were present.   The examination was very
thorough.   The answers given by the class were usu-
ally prompt and correct; but every now and then a
question was put that staggered them, and one after
another acknowledged his inability to answer it, until
it came to D.A. McGregor; and every time such a question came he struggled with it.   At such a time every
eye in the room was upon him, and the examiners
and professors were listening with deepest attention.
Dr. Fyfe and Dr. Cooper were sitting near me.   I
very well remember the satisfaction and pleasure
manifested in the countenances of these two brethren
when the answers were given.   In speaking with Dr.
Fyfe after the examination was over, I asked him if
Bro. McGregor had been as successful in the study of
other subjects as in the study of Theology.   He answered: 'He is a good student, he has made satisfactory progress in every subject he has taken up.'   I
expressed my great satisfaction with the examination
of the class and added that I was especially pleased
with the answers of Mr. McGregor and the intellectual power manifested therein.   'Yes,' said he, 'taking
him all in all he has the best mind yet given to us.'
After characterizing his mind as 'strong, clear and
well-balanced,' he expressed the hope that Mr. Mc-
Gregor might be long spared to serve the cause of
God."

One who was present gives the following account
of a conversation that occurred during the session of
the Ottawa Association at Thurso, about 1877: "It
was in the evening.   A number were sitting around

chatting over the day's work. Dr. Fyfe had spoken
on the subject so dear to his heart—Education—at
the evening meeting, and continued in the same strain.
In speaking of Woodstock the question came up as
to whom he would like to have succeed him in the
principalship in the event of his being compelled by
failing health to relinquish his work. Looking around,
he said, 'I would like to see D. A. McGregor principal.'"
It is probable that Dr. Fyfe often expressed himself
in this way; for on the occasion of Mr. McGregor's
appointment to the principalship a minister in a distant province wrote him, congratulating him on his
appointment and referring to "Dr. Fyfe's prophecy
and its fulfilment." Though Mr. McGregor was very
reticent on such matters, one in whom he confided re-
members his account of a conversation with Dr. Fyfe
shortly before he entered upon his University course.
As the two were journeying eastward from Woodstock
by rail to meet their Sunday appointments, " Dr. Fyfe
crossed over to Mr. McGregor's seat, sat beside him,
and asked him if he had decided as to his course for
the future. Mr. McGregor said he had decided to
take the metaphysical course in the University of
Toronto and after that he would probably take a pastorate. Dr. Fyfe was opposed to his students' spend-
ing time on a University course and Mr. McGregor
expected to receive counsel along the line of disap-
proval; but not so. Dr. Fyfe remained silent a few
moments and then said; 'Bro. McGregor, you know
my views on this matter, as a rule. In your case I
have come to think that you will be doing a wise

thing in taking the metaphysical course. Have you ever thought of teaching as a life-work ?' Mr. McGregor said he had not, and then the Doctor requested and urged that he should work with a view to teaching Theology, encouraging him with the statement that, in his opinion, he possessed peculiar fitness for such work, and suggesting the possibility of his some day taking up the work that he must soon relinquish. He was so given to underestimating himself, that such words from Dr. Fyfe were a grateful surprise to him, and years after Dr. Fyfe had passed away, and when Mr. McGregor was happily at work in a pastorate with no other thought than that the pastorate would be his life-work, he would refer to that conversation in the car, humbly grateful that one whom he so much revered should have cherished such thoughts concerning him."

When the chair of Homiletics in Toronto Baptist College became vacant in 1886, through the decision of Rev. J. W. A. Stewart, then pastor of the Hamilton church, to remain in the pastorate, the Faculty of Toronto Baptist College naturally felt deep solicitude as to the efficient filling of the position. At the close of a chapel service, Dr. Castle announced Mr. Stewart's decision, and asked, in an informal way, who would be the next man. One of the professors answered with much confidence and without hesitation, " D. A. McGregor." In this answer the other members of the Faculty concurred. The sentiments of the Faculty with reference to Mr. McGregor's fitness for the position were informally communicated to one or two members of the committee of the Senate, whose duty it was to take the initiative in the matter of filling vacancies. Here also the suggestion met with the heartiest approval. The recommendation was made by the committee at the April meeting of the Senate, and Mr. McGregor was unanimously nominated to the Board of Trustees. Just at this time a crisis had been reached in the history of Woodstock College. After prolonged conference between representatives of Woodstock College and of Toronto Baptist College, it had been decided, with the approval of Senator McMaster, that strenuous efforts should be made for the endowment and equipment of Woodstock College, and that one of the seven professorial salaries that Senator McMaster was paying in connection with Toronto Baptist College, should be used for the support of a principal at Woodstock. Professor Stewart's withdrawal left a Faculty of six. If one of the remaining professors should accept the principalship of Woodstock College, the chair of Homiletics could be filled, and the Board would unanimously appoint the nominee of the Senate. Strong pressure was brought to bear upon Prof. T. H. Rand, D.C.L., whose rich educational experience was thought to make him preëminently the man for the crisis, by Senator McMaster and others; and, though he was reluctant to relinquish his work in Toronto Baptist College, it was confidently expected that he would accept the Woodstock principalship. Meanwhile Mr. McGregor was for weeks kept in suspense. Sympathizing with him in what must have been a greater or less degree of anxiety, one of the professors wrote him imparting such information as he possessed with respect to the probability of a speedy settlement of the matter in favor of his appointment. In a letter by way of reply, Mr. McGregor expressed his gratitude for the interest and sympathy shown, and while not denying that the suspense was somewhat unpleasant, said that he was by no means weary of the pastorate, and that he could be content to continue in that work. He was no doubt strongly attracted by the professorship; but even after his nomination by the Senate he would probably have submitted without a murmur, had providential circumstances prevented his appointment, and would have continued the quiet, unassuming, devoted, self-sacrificing, wise, successful pastor that for years he had been. Dr. Rand's acceptance of the Woodstock principalship soon made Mr. McGregor's appointment certain; but the next meeting of the governing bodies of the College was deferred for some time and the suspense continued. His appointment was made with much confidence and heartiness, and believing that thus most efficiently he could serve his Master, he promptly accepted the position.

The chair of instruction to which he was at first called, that of Homiletics, was not that which he would probably have chosen, or for which his peculiar gifts and attainments best fitted him. But he cheerfully undertook the work and did it with complete success. In addition to the work of his own department Professor McGregor gave instruction, during the session 1886-'87, to classes in Rhetoric and Oratory

and in Mental Science.   By the next year Dr. W. N.
Clarke's resignation had reduced the Faculty to five
members.   At this juncture it was decided to extend
and systematize the College course in the interpretation of the English Bible, and Dr. MacVicar having
been placed in charge of this work, Professor McGregor was asked to take, in addition to his work in
Homiletics, the department of Apologetics, which had
formerly been assigned to Dr. MacVicar.   This department was no doubt far more in accord with his
tastes and aptitudes than that to which he was originally appointed.   He cheerfully accepted the burden,
and applied himself most diligently to the work of
the new department.   His mind was a highly metaphysical and logical one, and he felt entirely at home
in defending the truth against its adversaries and in
overthrowing the bulwarks of error.

  In 1888, Dr. Castle's health having already begun
to fail, a redistribution of the work of the College
was recommended by a committee of which Dr. Castle
was a member, and was determined upon by the Senate.   In this redistribution Professor McGregor was
requested to take the department of Systematic Theology in conjunction with Apologetics.   It is needless
to say that this change of work was wholly unsought
by Professor McGregor.   But none the less, he must
have felt that now at last he had the department in
which he was capable of doing the most efficient service, and to which he would gladly give the remainder
of his life.   He threw himself with great enthusiasm
into his work, and although he was permitted to labor

only for one brief year after the change had been made, it was a year of strenuous effort crowned with success.

From the first, Professor McGregor enjoyed the highest respect and esteem of Faculty and students. We all felt that we had among us one of the choicest spirits, a man of keen, penetrating, comprehensive intellect, of adequate scholarship, of profound convictions, of absolute loyalty to the truth, an unselfish, warm-hearted, thoroughly loveable man. The students were enthusiastic in their admiration. As Secretary of the Home Mission Society, he had much dealing with the students with reference to Home Mission work, and in this relation, as well as in others, he inspired the fullest confidence. When he led in the daily worship, or took part in the monthly missionary meetings of the College, it was with power and in demonstration of the Spirit. As a member of the Executive of the Fyfe Missionary Society, his counsel was always most helpful. In the meetings of the Faculty, while he showed no disposition to unduly urge his own views, and was for the first year or two more reticent than might have seemed desirable, it was soon evident that he had deep convictions of his own, and that he was ready at the right time to make his influence profoundly felt along the lines of educational policy. As a member of the Senate, he was fearless in advocating the views he had reached and in criticising what seemed to him unwise and harmful measures. The utterances of few members of that body carried with them more of weight than his.

5

Professor McGregor had an intense conviction of the supreme importance to the denomination and to the cause of Christ of the efficient maintenance of Toronto Baptist College. Any scheme that involved, or seemed to him to involve, a subordination of theological to other work, was sure to find in him a determined opponent. The theological course should, he thought, be made richer and broader; an adequate number of chairs should be maintained; and a library, not simply commensurate with the immediate needs of the students but so rich in sources as to furnish inducement for learned research, should be provided: such in brief was his policy as regards our work in theological education. Not that he for a moment doubted the value of academic and Arts work—few men had a higher appreciation than he had of literary culture in and for itself and especially as a preparation for theological study; but with him the first and most pressing duty of the denomination lay in making the best possible provision for the theological training of students for the ministry. He believed that suitable provision should be made for the theological instruction not simply of well endowed and well trained men, but of men of inferior ability and inferior literary culture as well. He felt deeply, as we all must feel, the urgent need of a large increase in the number of young men consecrating themselves to the work of the ministry and submitting themselves to the most thorough training within their reach. He shared with others the conviction that a far larger proportion of the best life in our churches should be

consecrated to the ministry; and he believed that
much could be accomplished in this direction by the
earnest, persistent efforts of professors, pastors and
others.   While he laid great stress on intellectual preparation for the work of the ministry, he laid even
greater stress on moral and spiritual preparation. The
slightest deviation from moral rectitude, or the slightest manifestation of any other than the highest and
noblest aims and motives, destroyed whatever satisfaction he would otherwise have felt in the most brilliant intellectual gifts.   Yet his keenness to detect
blemishes did not make him censorious or unsympa-
thetic.  On the contrary, when he perceived a fault in
a brother, he was impelled by a desire to do all in his
power, by sympathetic, helpful counsel, and by prayer
for and with him, to secure amendment.

As Home Mission Secretary, Professor McGregor
had become widely known and had been brought into
intimate relations with many ministers and active
layman throughout the country.   As he continued to
hold this position during the first two years of his
College career, he received frequent visits and still
more frequent letters from brethren and churches in
need of counsel.   Such labor, always cheerfully bestowed, could not fail to absorb much of his time and
strength.

While occupying the professor's chair he preached
almost as much as if he had been pastor.   He loved
the pulpit and did not have it in his heart to refuse
to his brethren in the ministry the help that they
were very ready to solicit.   Summer and winter,

almost without intermission, he toiled day and night, seven days in the week. Long before his health had perceptibly broken, he was earnestly warned against subjecting himself to such severe and constant strain. But, alas! the warning was not heeded. To the very last, his powerful will forced his exhausted and protesting body and mind to fulfil engagements that should never have been made.

When Dr. John H. Castle—renowned and venerable name!—had been led by declining health to resign the Principalship of Toronto Baptist College in the spring of 1889, all eyes seem to have been turned at once to Professor McGregor as the most available man for the position. It is a source of satisfaction to one of his colleagues to remember that, before he had heard it suggested by any one else, he expressed to members of the Senate his conviction that, under all the circumstances, this would be the best appointment that could be made. His deep convictions as to the importance of the theological work, the high esteem in which he was held by Faculty and students, his thorough acquaintance with the denomination and its needs, and the large measure of confidence that was accorded to him by his brethren throughout the denomination, along with the gifts and graces that qualified him for the Professor's chair, made it certain that his appointment to the Principalship would be hailed with delight by the constituency of the College. This expectation was more than realized. There was general rejoicing that the position which Dr. Castle had so ably and successfully filled was henceforth to be occupied by this rising young Canadian theologian. Letters flowed in upon him from all parts of Canada, and from several places in the United States, expressive of the highest satisfaction. The enthusiasm of the students was unbounded. Alas! what seemed to be the opening up of a most brilliant and useful career as leader in the theological education of our denomination in Canada was really the end of a short but singularly beautiful and useful life of Christian service.

The loss of his only son, an attractive and promising child of three years, in the summer of 1888, was a severe blow to Professor McGregor. This, along with other sorrows and anxieties, almost prostrated him, and the College year of 1888-'89 was thus one of consuming toil amid manifold trials and afflictions. The strain on his nervous system must have been enormous. The disease that finally proved fatal must have been already doing its secret work, and was no doubt aggravated by overwork and anxiety. Those who were with him from day to day could see only too plainly that he was " burning the candle at both ends." What seemed to be an iron constitution gave way. The last illness and death of the beloved Principal shall be described in another chapter.

The following description of Mr. McGregor's private life during this period could only have been written by one who shared with him day by day the joys and the sorrows of life: " At the time of his appointment to the Principalship and several times after—once or twice while lying in the hospital—he said ' one of the happiest thoughts to me in connection with this appointment is this: I will now be in a position, influentially and financially, to do something for the aged men in our denomination. I do so long to see them so placed that their declining years will not be made painful by want and dependence upon others. He said, that at our Conventions, where young men were pressing to the front, and so few old men were heard, he often felt oppressed with the fear that we might become so engrossed in educational and missionary interests as to forget the fathers in Israel—a most serious calamity.

"He loved the students, and entered with all his heart into everything that tended to their advancement and welfare. It pains me to think how he labored day and night, year after year, never resting, but searching constantly for rich mines of truth into which he might bring his students. I can truthfully say that every lecture which he delivered in McMaster Hall cost him many hours of close application to work. He never went before the students with any but the most careful preparation. He depended little, if at all, on the writings of others; his lectures, in Theology especially, being wrought out by himself, Bible in hand. He stood very near to the students in sympathy—sympathy with them as young men and as students. He desired to be helpful to them in every possible way. To this end he would visit them in their rooms, invite them to walk with him or to visit him in his home. Often when I would ask him if he was at liberty to walk with me in the afternoon

or evening he would say, 'I can't to-day,—Mr. A. is
astray on the communion question, and I have asked
him to walk with me to-night. I want to set him
right,' or 'Mr. B. is depressed, thinks he isn't called to
the ministry, and I have asked him over to talk about
it.' Only himself and the students whom he thus
helped knew how he worked along such lines. One
of the most touching incidents in his long illness was
just before his departure for New York. The students
had a prayer meeting in his room; after the meeting
a number lingered to say to him—some with tears—
how helpful he had been to them. After they had
gone from the room I went in, and he said eagerly :
'G——, these young men have spoken strange words
to me to-night. . . . G——, do they mean it, or
is it just because I'm sick and they want to say kind
things' ? He longed to be helpful to them, but hardly
dared to hope that he had been so. Yet while striving
to be thus helpful, he was careful to avoid any show
of familiarity or any sacrifice of the dignity which he
felt belonged by right to the teacher. It was his firm
conviction that when students began to place themselves on the same level with the teacher, patronizing
rather than respecting him, they and he had better
part company. I believe every student yielded him
the profoundest respect even while confiding in him
as in an elder brother. They wrote to him individu-
ally and in a body, while he lay in the hospital, always
assuring him of their regard for him and of their earnest desire that God would restore him to them."

A sketch of Mr. McGregor's career as Theological

Professor and Principal should contain some expression, in their own words, of the sentiments and impressions of those for whose advancement he so earnestly and so unsparingly labored. Several of those who for two or three years enjoyed daily intercourse with him in the class-room and were objects of his constant care out of the class-room as well, have furnished us with written statements of the impressions left upon them by our departed brother. To insert these statements in full would unduly extend this chapter; selection and condensation, therefore, must needs be resorted to.

A former student writes: "I regarded Mr. McGregor as a safe man, because his cast of thought was, in my opinion, neither unduly conservative nor unduly rationalistic, and further because his intimate personal acquaintance with our denomination qualified him to speak without a peradventure about those things which our churches needed. I often admired his power to make clear-cut distinctions and nice discriminations in the subjects which we handled. He was, however, more than a cold thinker. He not only thought out the system of doctrines upon which he lectured, but he felt their power, and falling tears often evinced his emotion while he spoke of some particular aspect of the truth. This made us all feel that we had before us not only a theological professor but also a Christian man whose life was swayed by the great principles about which he spoke. I find it hard to estimate the value of such a view of Christian doctrines. He must be a brilliant botanist who can not only give to his students a strictly accurate scien-

tific knowledge of flowers, but can also inspire in
them an enthusiastic admiration for their æsthetic
beauty. This was what Professor McGregor succeeded
in doing. He not only made us see the truth, but he
made us feel its power, and perceive its beauty. I
found him however to be more than a professor. He
was a personal friend. In cases when I needed advice
he was ready, very ready, to give it. In one case in
particular—a case of peculiar difficulty, I availed myself of his readiness to help, and I feel that his clear
and careful advice aided largely in the successful management of a very difficult matter. In this respect I
have more than ordinary reason for gratitude, since,
as I am informed, one of the last occasions on which
he left his house was when he went to secure for me
some information which my pastoral work required.
In short, I have met very few men who have better
deserved that very high encomium pronounced on
Brutus in *Julius Cæsar:*

> His life was gentle, and the elements
> So mixed in him, that Nature might stand up
> And say, this was a man !"

Another: "As a lecturer on Homiletics, New Testament Interpretation and Apologetics he was always
helpful and satisfactory ; but in my opinion it was in
the work of Systematic Theology that he found his
element and rendered his most distinguished service.
I consider that Professor McGregor's distinguishing
characteristic as a teacher was *his insistence upon accurate definitions.* This he demanded of himself and
sought from his classes. With him the first thing in

teaching was definition and the second thing was definition and the third thing was definition. He never left a subject until he showed how it was differentiated from others closely related to it. I believe it was to his felicity in definition that his success as a teacher was largely due. Another noteworthy characteristic was his *unvarying patience*. He never grew impatient with a slow and feeble thinker. If he found one of his class in any perplexity he would take the utmost pains to determine the cause and afford relief Sometimes after leading us, as he supposed, along an easy path to a desired point he would find that some careless one had strayed into a by-path and got caught among the brambles. Yet he would retrace his steps and bring up the delinquent so tenderly and lovingly that he would almost feel tempted to repeat the offense. Professor McGregor taught us not only systematic *theology* but systematic *Christianity*. I might also mention his *winsomeness*. Perhaps this is involved in what has gone before : but I would like to emphasize it. He was a winsome teacher. I sometimes wonder whether teachers realize what a great thing it is to gain the hearts of their students. Professor McGregor won our love and made us desirous of winning his approbation."

Another : "Humility was a prominent characteristic in his life and bearing. This is shown by his cool reception of a warm congratulation accorded him on his becoming Principal. Sincerity was another of his virtues. He was just what he appeared to be, despising all forms of hypocrisy, as is shown by the following circumstance : in a letter to the graduating class, shortly before his death, he strongly warned them never to preach for popularity or emolument, but to seek some other calling, if their great object was not the salvation of souls. The student felt that he had not only an able teacher but also a loving friend who was deeply interested in all his plans and prospects, and who thoroughly sympathized with the student's arduous struggles with poverty and inexperience. Also may be mentioned his unselfishness in Christian giving, loyalty to principle in not accepting ministers' exemptions, absence of a self-seeking spirit which is ever striving for position and advancement, affability and kindness to all. He was a spiritually-minded, meek and trustful disciple of the Lord Jesus. He strongly impressed the student with his devotional attitude even in dealing with the most abstruse theological problems. His Christlike spirit, growth in grace, and submission to whatever the Holy Spirit pointed out as God's will, are prominent factors in his character. The latter quality is shown in his offer to go to India. He was a wonderfully clear-headed, logical thinker. He took a firm grip on truth, and possessed the remarkable power of plucking the kernel of truth from the husk and shell of confusion surrounding it. Not only could he clearly conceive, but he could also briefly, pointedly and forcibly express the truth. His language was elegant and appropriate and sounded as if previously studied, so well placed was every word. He did not use superfluous words. His mind was both destructive and constructive. As a teacher he was clear, systematic, thorough, slow to cover ground, encouraging independent thinking. He paid much attention to the connection of the different parts of Scripture, and to particles, such as, for, therefore, etc. He treated his students not as children but as men; he did not tear to pieces every thought to which they might give utterance, in order to get up a discussion, and leave them at the end of the lecture with nothing to carry away."

Another writes: "The memory of Professor McGregor shall ever be cherished by me as one of the brightest reminiscences in my College life. It must ever prove an inspiration for good. I have always felt that to come into his presence was to come under the sway of a master spirit. He seemed to be able with ease to enter into our difficult and perplexing problems, placing himself as it were in the student's place, and then with a look of pain, mingled with the tenderest sympathy, he would unfold to us his explanation and way out of the difficulty. At the same time he gave to us the most agreeable consciousness of our own powers and faculties expanding to the light like the morning flowers. He never seemed to dictate, yet his powers of presenting his views were such that his opinions and judgments were the most easy and delightful to harmonize. It seemed almost like presumption to question his position, or oppose his views, which of course we sometimes did. His decision of character was marked. In every subject he undertook to discuss he was firm and decided, thoroughly prepared to meet attack from every quarter. At the same time there was perfect freedom from arrogance in the announcement of his positions, of which he appeared to be absolutely confident.

"Moreover, this firmness of character was always tempered with a mildness and tenderness of manner which is rarely possessed by humanity. He was always one of the most unselfish of men. The memory of his life and character must ever prove an incentive and an encouragement to holiness and consecration. The accompanying lines, which I have had in my possession for a long time, very fully express my sentiments and impression of Professor McGregor. I do not know where I got them, nor who the author is.

Ah ! how shall we proclaim his worth,
  His virtues how unfold ?
Of tender thoughts there is no dearth,
  But written words are cold.

A meek and holy spirit set
  A modest shrine within,
And eloquence whose pleading yet
  Ne'er failed our hearts to win.

A mantle of humility
  That's never cast aside,
A heart where truth and dignity
  And charity abide.

A soul in which a constant flame
  Of love for men burned clear ;
In whose pure light a selfish aim
  Ignoble did appear.

These gifts in perfect union blent
  Have cast a wondrous spell,
And many hearts to-day are rent
  With grief too deep to tell.

But in their voiceless depth will sleep
  One germ as strong as death,
A memory that will freshness keep
  While love has life and breath."

Another: "I wish I could analyse the causes that made me love Professor McGregor better than any man other than my father. His qualification for success was not so much his teaching power as his beautiful character. He was preëminently pious, and yet his piety was not self-assertive but evidently genuine. He was loving. His knowledge of the students and their hopes and fears was not acquired from a sense of duty but from real interest. He believed in us too. Our weaknesses did not cause his anger but awoke a longing to help us, while earnest purpose caused him real joy. He was bold and never shrank from examining his belief from foundation to coping, nor was he afraid to consider a new interpretation of Scriptural passages. If a student sought to enter the realms of dangerous thought he did not hold him back but went with him and guided him. He had abundance of animal spirits, his gladness was overflowing. Thus his life was symmetrical. To live under its influence was like breathing a pure spiritual air, if I may so speak. His earnestness was a constant inspiration, and so thoroughly permeated all his actions that little details received as much attention as larger things."

Another: "Among the many qualities possessed by him whom I had the privilege of knowing as more than an ordinary friend were two that should be specially noted in reference to his work in the professoriate. First, there was the power he possessed of *enlisting the confidence* of the students and others with whom he had to do. His Christian manliness,

his undoubted ability, his genuine sympathy, all contributed to inspire one with confidence in him, and
thus proved a help to him and to those in any way
related to him. Another quality worthy of mention
was the *patience and interest he manifested* when
listening to the opinions and convictions of those
whom he taught. However meagre might be the
thoughts of the students in his classes they always
received the attention and respect of the professor.
No student was ever 'crushed' by him because of
difference of opinion. He ever sought in a manly and
Christian way to lead into what he believed to be
the light."

Another writes: "I was glad when the appointment came to a position in the College, and I began
no College year with more readiness and liking than
that second year of my course. We had not got back
to work very long before he came to me (I suspect
because of our previous acquaintance) and wished to
know all he could about the work of his classes from
a student's standpoint. He then told me of the hopes
he cherished regarding the work. The ideal he had
was far above the mere teaching of prescribed lessons
so many days a week. He wrought to get us to see the
honor of our work, and the spirit we should cherish
in the doing of it. I will not forget how he set himself to find out the best way in which he could be
helpful to us. It was always a precious hour when
he came to visit our rooms, for he not only interested
himself in the studies we had, but he also took the
deepest interest in the health of the spiritual life.

There was no trouble ever showed itself in our faces, but his eye saw, and he became not only a sympathetic brother, but also a wise and loving father in counsel."

Another: "Strange as it may seem, in view of the readiness of students to speak out what they think, or in short to grumble, I never heard a complaint of Professor McGregor, and more and more his word was coming to be regarded as law."

Another: "I always admired and revered him on account of his great power, mental, spiritual and as a teacher; also for his kindly and devotional spirit in the class-room and everywhere. Tears would often fill his eyes as he discussed some point in theology with us. The solemn relation of every truth to the weal or woe of man seemed ever present in his mind and heart, and he travailed in birth, so to speak, till the same mind should be formed in us. His last hour with us in the Senior Theology class was a fitting and natural close to the College career. After about a half hour's lecture he called on three members of the class to engage successively in prayer. When these had done he prayed himself. His prayer was so searching, so touching, that I think every one of us left the room in tears."

Another: "His loving nature, his friendly disposition, the wisdom of his counsel, and his unquestionable ability have made impressions on my mind that time cannot obliterate. . . . I was greatly impressed with his ability to repeat the word of God."

Another: "The unassuming, Christlike grandeur of his character, the amiability of his deportment, the vigor and rugged, forceful logic of his intellect, his thorough mastery of the most difficult theological problems, his book-like precision of statement in elucidating these problems, his student-like geniality, his approachable disposition, coupled with his unassertive firmness, have left an impression upon me which the wreckings of time shall never obliterate. Few such personalities grace the canvas of a single generation."

The following letters, written by Principal McGregor in St. Luke's hospital, New York, shortly before his death, and addressed, the one to the acting Principal, the Faculty and the students of Toronto Baptist College, and the other to the Graduating Class of 1890, show how deep was his solicitude even to the last for the College, and how anxious he was that the students should keep proper ideals before them :—

" I have not written to you hitherto because I knew you would have information regarding my condition from Mrs. McGregor. She has not reached New York yet, but I hope to see her within a couple of hours.

" You will notice by place of date that I have changed hospitals. The reason is that I asked Dr. Abbe to operate in my case. Dr. Weir, whom I expected to perform the operation, is now in Europe, but I am quite as well satisfied with the present arrangement. I am to have my spine opened next Wednesday.

" I know that I am nearing a great crisis. I am not confident as to how it may go with me ; yet in my condition of growing helplessness I think I am justified in accepting the risk. I know you all have been

6

praying for me and I thank you very sincerely for this. I know you will pray for me and for those whose burden will be very heavy should it go ill with me.

"I trust that through the infinite mercy of God in Christ I shall be able to face the approaching issues without fear; yet I have a very strong desire to live and labor with you. I confess that I would like to have a better filled day of service ere I go home. Perhaps God may grant me this desire.

"My dear young brethren, believe in the Gospel of Jesus Christ with all your hearts, and give yourselves as living sacrifices to Him, that He may work through you mightily in life's brief day. O let nothing turn you aside from the great work to which you have given your lives, and in that work let no motive have place that would not stand the light of the all-manifesting day.

"Now, dear teachers and students, farewell. I have loved you and shall continue so to do. I have loved to labor with you and perhaps this joy may even yet be restored to me. But, if not, His will be done.

"I will not write more to-day. I wish you all the bliss of Christ's service on earth and his glory in heaven.

"Your fellow-laborer,
"D. A. McGregor."


"DEAR BRETHREN,—I received your welcome letter yesterday, and thank you for the thoughtful kindness that prompted you to send it, as well as for the warm sympathy and assurance of kindly regard which it contained. I thank you too for your photographs, with which, Mrs. McGregor informs me, you have favored us.

"I think you know how I hoped and longed to spend at least a part of this year with you in class-room work. This desire did not arise from the thought that I might impart something to you which you have not otherwise obtained. I wished, if possible, through continued intercourse, especially in the last year of your College work, to cement more closely a friendship, which might bind us together in a brotherhood of service for Christ however distanced we might be one from another in the field of toil; yet I trust, my brethren, if future of life and service on earth may be mine, that you will permit me to stand not less closely to your lives than if I had had the opportunity I desired of daily fellowship with you in your efforts to gain further fitness for the great life-work that opens up before you in the realm of Gospel enterprise.

"My brethren, I know that I may now be writing farewell words to you, and what shall I say? Be true to the ministry which you have received of the Lord Jesus. Let the power of the great unselfish life come more and more into your own lives. The worst of all disasters that can possibly overtake you is that you should stand at the end of life having made shipwreck of the greatest trust that was ever committed to creature life—the preaching of the Gospel of the Grace of God.

"Never, never, *never* use the cross of Christ to exalt yourselves. If any are ambitious of self-display, O

let them choose other themes than the Gospel, and
other places than the pulpit and the church of God.
Let the same mind be in you which was also in Christ
Jesus, who made Himself of *no reputation.* Adorn
the Gospel you proclaim with its own matchless graces
in-wrought in your lives. O ! glad at the end of
life's brief day will you all be if you have not sought
your own things, but the things of Jesus Christ. I
pray for you, my brethren. May you all have a very
fruitful ministry, and may your work abide. May
Jesus say to each one of you as He greets you beyond
the shores of the present life, 'Well done, good and
faithful servant.'

"And now, my dear brethren, farewell. I thank
you for your kind letter ; it has cheered me. I thank
you for your prayerful remembrance of me during all
these months. I thank you for the kindness you have
shown to Mrs. McGregor in the long season of painful
anxiety. The God of power and grace and comfort
bless you all.

"Yours in the everlasting bonds,<br>"D. A. McGregor."

The words in which John Gerson, the famous
Chancellor of the University of Paris about the
beginning of the fifteenth century, characterized
Bonaventura, "the Seraphic Doctor," may fittingly
be applied to D. A. McGregor : "If I were asked, who
among other teachers seems more capable, I should
reply without prejudice, Master Bonaventura, since he
is solid and safe in teaching, pious, just and devout.

Moreover, he recedes as far as possible from vain curiosity, not mingling extraneous positions, or doctrines secular, dialectical or philosophical, shadowed over with theological terms, after the manner of many, but, while he diligently seeks the illumination of the intellect, he refers everything to piety and to producing a right condition of the heart. . . . No teaching is for theologians more sublime, none more divine, none more salubrious and agreeable."

> " Fearlessly glad he walked in Truth's highway
> Who joined him there, had fellow stout to cheer ;
> Who crossed, met foe behooved his weal to fear ;
> His quick, keen, urgent, sinewy, certain thrust
> Those knights well knew who felt it in the joust.
> Ideal-Christian teacher, master, man,
> Severely sweet, a gracious Puritan,
> Beyond my praise to-day, beyond their blame,
> He spurs me yet with his remembered name."

W. C. WILKINSON.

# CHAPTER V.

A.D. 1880-'90.

When, in the autumn of 1870, the subject of this memoir exchanged a sphere of physical labor in the open air for one of secluded and mental toil, he was possessed of rugged bodily health and strength; and, excepting for a few days upon a single occasion in early boyhood, he had never been seriously ill. His physical vigor enabled him to endure the strain of so radical a change in his way of life, begun at so advanced a period of his youth, and involving severe and protracted application, much better than might have been expected. Apart from an attack somewhat of the nature of nervous prostration, lasting for several months in the summer and autumn of 1872, his health suffered no material injury during his career as a student; and though heavily freighted, for a large part of the time, with the extra work of preaching and pastoral care—which was necessary to his maintenance — he completed his literary and theological studies in Woodstock, April 1878, and his University course in Toronto, May 1881, considerably exhausted, indeed, but apparently without damage to his constitution.

From this time forward, through all his manifold labors as pastor, Home Mission secretary, and theological professor, his health remained sound and good, excepting that about once a year, for a number of years previous to his last illness, he suffered severe " bilious " attacks, in which not merely bile, but dark blood also, was thrown off from the stomach, and which were always attended with several hours of hiccough. But firmly believing that he was a man of exceptionally strong constitution and vigorous health, and that sickness and medicine were not for him, he did not consult a physician about the matter, nor attach any importance to it whatever.

This ailment, however, trivial though it seemed to the subject of it, may have been the reason of Divine Providence in suddenly and utterly expunging from his mind both the purpose and the desire of going as a missionary to India, which for a time he had seriously entertained ; for, an eminent physician, to whom the symptoms were casually mentioned by a friend, said, " that man could never live in India." Not that this occasional stomachic disturbance weighed an atom with the subject of it, in his decision of the question ; for, unfortunately, it was never a matter of more than the slightest consequence : but during the progress of a Foreign Mission meeting held in Woodstock in 1885, to which he went with the intention of offering himself for the work, clear and satisfying light broke in upon his mind and firmly and finally convinced him that he ought not to take the step, but to continue his work for the Master in Canada. That this same ail-

ment, however, should reappear, after a year's absence,
at the very time when he was rapidly and hopefully
convalescing from a critical surgical operation and by
the persistent hiccough, which the affection always induced, should combine with other incidental ailments
to weary and wear the life out of him, is one of the
strangest and saddest of sad and strange things.

Early in July 1886, when a heavy piano was being
moved into his house in Toronto, he went under it to
adjust the pedal, when, accidentally, it was let down
upon him with a great part of its weight, giving a
violent wrench to his back, though after a few days
he felt no ill effects from it. Six months later, when
shoving the same instrument across a room, he was
seized with an excruciating pain, at the same point
in the back. This, also, soon passed away; but, in
the judgment of eminent physicians who studied his
case, these accidents were the primary cause of the
spinal disease in his last illness.

The sudden death of his only, his bright and in-
tensely-loved little son, Arthur, in September 1888,
was a most crushing and perilous blow to his highly
susceptible organization. Important changes occur-
ring about this time and at a later period in his work
as professor taxed his strength to the full during the
next College year. For several months previous to
the middle of June 1889 he was overwhelmingly bur-
dened with anxiety over a peculiarly terrible domestic
calamity that was threatening and imminent. In a
letter written about that time he speaks of it as " a
strain of anxiety beyond expression." Through these

later circumstances, his strength was much run down when his last illness began to take possession of him.

Sometime in June 1889, he began to complain of a peculiar pain in his back. By the first of July it had considerably increased, and was attended with some loss of power in the evacuative organs. On seeking advice, he was thought to be suffering simply from muscular rheumatism, and was treated accordingly, but without relief. It soon became difficult for him to move about, or to do mental work; yet on Lord's Day evening July 14th, at one of the opening services in the Parkdale church, Toronto, he preached a tender and impressive gospel sermon, which proved, however, to be his last. His text on this occasion was the Saviour's saying in John vi: 37, "Him that cometh unto me I will in no wise cast out." The sermon was spoken of as "simple, affectionate, earnest"; as strongly contrasting "the one coming and the One to whom he comes"; as emphasizing the welcome extended by the Saviour and the impossibility of his rejecting a sinner who comes to him; as appealing earnestly to the unconverted to accept of Christ; "and thus," says one, "in keeping with the character of our brother, was closed his last service of intense love for, and sympathy with those who were in need." Though weak and in pain, he walked from the College to the service and back, thinking that perhaps the exercise might benefit him; but all through the service he suffered greatly, and he reached home distressed and exhausted.

The pains in his back, and the loss of power, already

referred to, continued to increase; and loss of power and of control in the use of his lower limbs soon became manifest, and made such marked progress that shortly he was led to suspect that something more serious than had been supposed, possibly some spinal affection, might be the matter with him. Thus with weakness and pain, aggravated by doubt and apprehension, the time in the sick-room dragged wearily on.

But one sad night, near the end of August, while alone in his chamber bravely endeavoring to carry out urgent advice to take exercise, which he did by sliding chairs about while leaning on them for support, he fell prostrate and was unable to rise. The next day, after a medical consultation, his disease was pronounced paralysis. Complete paralysis of the lower half of the body had set in, and for a few days he lay at the point of death. On Sunday morning, the third day after the crash, he thought himself, and was thought by all who were about him, to be upon the very point of departure; and, being in a state of mental and spiritual exaltation, he took a peculiarly tender and affecting farewell of his loved and loving family and friends. But the event was ordered otherwise, and, for the time being, his life was spared.

His paralysis remained unchanged, but his strong vitality asserted itself, and enabled him in a few weeks to regain a goodly measure of strength in the upper half of his body and to use his mind vigorously, and with as much originality and clearness as ever.

Through the kindness and liberality of the Board

of Governors of the College, an eminent specialist in nervous diseases, Dr. Seguin, of New York, was sent for, about the middle of October, to examine and pronounce upon his condition and prospects, and to recommend a course of treatment. After sifting the history and symptoms of the case, and applying the requisite tests, he came to the decided and encouraging conclusion that the paralysis was not caused, as had been feared, by myelitis, that is, inflammation and deterioration of the spinal cord, but to Potts' disease, a tubercular affection of spinal bone and not of spinal marrow, a disease far more amenable to treatment, often cured by proper mechanical appliances skilfully employed, and sometimes, latterly, when all else failed, by surgical operations upon the spine. Dr. Seguin strongly hoped that, by thorough use of such means and remedies as he recommended, recovery might soon be secured; but, if these should fail, he advised that the patient be sent to New York, that he might undergo, at the hands of the first surgeons of the day, an operation in spinal surgery. It is but fair to say that the specialist's diagnosis was subsequently confirmed by the most eminent surgeons in New York, and demonstrated in the process of surgical operation.

During the many weeks of waiting in vain for recovery before leaving his home for a hospital in New York, the mind of the patient was unclouded and active, and ranged and ruminated freely over a variety of important subjects—sociological, metaphysical, poetical, theological and spiritually experimental.

Not long before his great illness set in he had been appointed to prepare, and to read before the Baptist Congress of 1889, a paper on the "Authority of Christian Consciousness," a subject which interested him deeply, and for which his metaphysical talents and attainments specially qualified him. To his very great disappointment he was prevented by his disabled condition from attempting the task.

Among his sick-bed papers there has been found a small pocket memorandum-book, which, among other matters, contains a few hasty jottings on the subject, almost illegible because of abbreviations and the unsteadiness of a bed-ridden hand, which were evidently designed merely for the jogging of his memory and for suggestion in research should he ever again be well enough to take hold of the subject. These rough and fragmentary notes indicate, at least to those who read between the lines, somewhat of the bent of his mind, the temper of his intellect, and his eager desire for work even when in the grasp of a fell disease.

Had it pleased God to spare his life and restore his health, there seems reason to believe that, sooner or later, he would have had something important to say on this subject.

In close and in rather unusual harmony with the philosophic faculty, there was in him also a poetic vein, how extensive and fertile cannot now be known, but of whose genuineness and fineness there is some positive evidence in the fragments that he has left behind. Shortly before leaving home for the last time alive it was noticed by his affectionate wife that his mind was joyfully simmering over some subject very precious to him, and that with tenderly playful secrecy he was silently concealing from her the mental product while in course of preparation. He was composing a hymn expressive of adoring love and ardent longing for the Saviour. For its own sake and for the sake of indicating the lofty spiritual experiences of soul which in latter years had been his, and which specially characterized the last months of his life, it is now placed in the narrative :—

Jesus, wondrous Saviour !
  Christ, of kings the King !
Angels fall before Thee,
  Prostrate, worshipping ;
Fairest they confess Thee
  In the heaven above.
We would sing Thee fairest,
  Here in hymns of love.

Fairer far than sunlight
  Unto eyes that wait,
Amid fear and darkness,
  Till the morning break.
Fairer than the day-dawn,
  Hills and dales among,
When its tide of glory
  Wakes the tide of song.

Sweeter far than music
  Quivering from keys
That unbind all feeling
  With strange harmonies,
Thou art more and dearer
  Than all minstrelsy,
Only in Thy presence
  Can joy's fulness be.

All earth's flowing pleasures
  Were a wintry sea ;
Heaven itself without Thee
  Dark as night would be.

Lamb of God !  Thy glory;
  Is the light above;
Lamb of God !  Thy glory
  Is the life of love.

Life is death, if severed
  From Thy throbbing heart,
Death with life abundant
  At Thy touch would start.
Worlds and men and angels
  All consist in Thee ;
Yet Thou comest to us
  In humility.

Jesus ! all perfections
  Rise and end in Thee,
Brightness of God's glory
  Thou, eternally.
Favor'd beyond measure
  They Thy face who see ;
May we, gracious Saviour,
  Share this ecstasy.

No relief whatever from the paralysis having come
during two and a half months after Dr. Seguin's visit,
the patient, in accordance with further advice from
him, was taken to New York in order to receive treatment, mainly through mechanical appliances at the
hands of orthopedic experts, and, if thereafter it should
be deemed necessary, to undergo a surgical operation.

He arrived on the 28th day of December, the eighth
and, in view of the strange and trying circumstances,
a not very joyous anniversary of his marriage.

It was arranged that he should receive treatment
under the care and oversight of the celebrated Dr.
R. S. Weir, Surgeon in New York Hospital, and Con-
sulting Surgeon in St. Luke's ; and, if a surgical
operation should become necessary, that it should be
performed by his hands.

As all the private rooms of the New York Hospital were occupied, Dr. Weir kindly managed to procure him one in St. Luke's; but in order to reduce expenses to a minimum, which the severe pecuniary drain of the long illness rendered necessary, it was soon determined to exchange it for a bed in a ward. In order that the patient might be more immediately under the supervision of Dr. Weir, and that, at the same time, he might have the benefit of the orthopedic skill of Dr. Adoniram B. Judson, a son of the great missionary, the patient, after a week's residence in St. Luke's was removed, January 4th (1890), to a ward in the New York Hospital, where he remained till March 13th. During the nearly ten weeks of his stay in that hospital, Dr. Judson attended him with the greatest fidelity and tenderness, and exhausted the possibilities of orthopedic appliances in his behalf: and he could not be persuaded to make a charge for his services, though they did not belong to the internal economy of the institution.

Life in the surgical ward of a crowded hospital in a great city was, at first, a startlingly strange experience for our invalid; and it presented to him many new and suggestive phases of human character and existence. It can scarcely be regarded as an ideal kind of life, for an earnest Christian man, of positive and solemn beliefs concerning the future state, of quick sensibilities and sympathies, to lie, himself a helpless sufferer, in a large room filled with suffering patients, not always patient sufferers—many of them about to undergo, many of them having recently undergone, surgical operations, which, taken together, varied in kind and degree, from the ordinary to the most severe and terrible—some of them recovering and departing to their homes; others of them succumbing, and departing, prepared or unprepared, to the eternal world. Nevertheless, it brought to the sick one, whose fortunes we are following, the merciful compensation of drawing him out of himself and of relieving him from the pains and perils of habitual and excessive introspection. During a considerable part of his hospital life, he was able to enjoy the reading of books, the visits of friends, and the reading, and to some extent the writing, of letters. His attendants, in both hospitals, took great and kindly interest in him. He was much cheered and comforted many a time by the visits of Rev. Dr. J. F. Elder, Rev. Dr. Edward Judson, Rev. Leighton Williams, Rev. John L. Campbell, and other persons of New York; and of Mr. Thomas Leeming and Rev. A. P. McDiarmid of Brooklyn; and it need scarcely be said that his relatives resident in the former city regard it as a great providential favor that it was possible for them to be much at his bedside.

The condition of the patient, instead of improving, grew worse. The paralysis was not relieved in any degree whatever, and the dangerous kidney and bladder disorders consequent upon the paralysis became more and more serious and unmanageable; and so acute were they at times that, on two occasions during his stay in New York Hospital, they very nearly swept him away. As these secondary complaints could not be overcome except by the cure of the paralysis, and as it had become manifest that the paralysis could not be cured except by surgical interference, and as there was considerable ground of hope, in the nature of things and in the history of several recent cases, that by this means his life might be spared and his health restored, he became thoroughly convinced that it was his duty at no distant day to submit to an operation.

In all circumstances and vicissitudes his heart was constantly set upon his distant home; and his love and longing for his family, from whom never before had he been much separated, were now often painfully intense and tender. One who witnessed can never forget the inexpressible and overpowering gratitude and joy with which he received the news of the conversion of his first-born child. It may perhaps be well here to take the reader into confidence and partly to draw aside the veil from the most sacred affections of the husband and father. Accordingly some letters to his wife and children are now given; to which a few to other relatives are added.

These and other letters from him reveal, besides his tender love and concern for his family, his firm trust in Christ, his great desire to live for Christ's service, his profound submission to the will of God whatever it might prove to be, and his resolution and courage in facing the dread ordeal awaiting him.

DEAR WIFE:

Your letter telling me of Edith's experience reached me and gladdened me last night. It has
left me all broken up in feeling since I read it, and
re-read it, but I would not be without the brokenness,
for it is gladness. I trust her experience is conversion
—her *conscious* acceptance of and yielding to Christ
as Saviour and Lord. And yet, there has been a good
deal in Edith's life which has led me to think that
her regeneration had been wrought, and was the hidden cause of much that lay half concealed and half
revealed, in her anxious little life. God grant that
the light that has arisen upon her may shine more
and more unto the perfect day. O how thankful we
should be, if He makes our little ones, in their early
youth, His own—the gems of His kingdom. . . . .

D. A.

MY DEAR, DEAR EDITH:

I received a letter from mamma last night and
it was nearly all about you. She was telling me of
the talk you and she had on Sunday night after you
came home from church, and how you believe that
now you have begun to be a Christian. My dear little
Edith, I have read that letter over and over again and
have cried with gladness every time I read it. O
Edith, how I long to put my arms round you and
draw you to my heart and kiss you and talk to you
and you to me about your becoming a Christian.

Some day God may let us meet again and then we will talk much about it. I am praying for you, Edith, that you may be a very happy and a very useful Christian. I am sure it will make you happy to know that God loves you and that Jesus is your friend, near to you every day and every night, and that he has given you a new heart to trust and love and serve him, and that you are saved because he died for you. You can be happier now when you play, or study, or rest, and Jesus will help you in everything to do what is right. Yet you will often find, dear Edith, that Satan will tempt you to do wrong, perhaps to get angry, perhaps to want to have your own way too much. Sometimes he may tempt you to be selfish, perhaps to quarrel with Gertie or to think that mamma does not love you because she does not let you do anything you want to, and in many other ways Satan will tempt you. But, dear Edith, Jesus is stronger far than Satan, and He is always ready to help you whenever you ask him, and when you forget and do wrong he will gladly forgive you, if you with sorrow for the wrong, go to him and ask him to forgive you. I know that you will try to be a true Christian, and be happy and loving, and obedient, and trustful, all the day. I am glad that you are going to try to help Gertie to be a Christian ; and O I shall be so glad to know that dear little Gertie has become a Christian too. I wish I were near you both and well again so that I could help you ; but I know that Jesus is always with you ; and he can and will help you far more than I can. Dear little ones, may He ever lead you and may you ever follow His leading, and be

saved from all the dangers of life.  It is so good to
become a Christian when you are young; for then by
serving Jesus from day to day you will be saved from
many bad habits and many temptations.  Now, my
Edith, you belong to Jesus.  You are more His than
mine.  You will never break your word to Him, that
from this time you will trust and love and serve Him,
and He will never break His word to you that He will be
with you always, that He will never leave you.  I shall
be glad to hear from you.  You can tell mamma what
you want her to write—if you find it happy to be a
Christian, if you are able to help Gertie any, and if
you find that Jesus helps you.  I will be glad, Edith,
if you will pray for papa that God may make him
well if it is best, and that he may help me to be a
better Christian day by day.  Will you kiss mamma
and auntie and Gertie and Enid for me; and mamma
will kiss you for me.

Dear Edith, I have been made very glad by mamma's letter which told me that you now are a Christian.  I pray and hope that some day I may see you.

With much love to my dear little Edith.

PAPA.

MY DEAR WIFE:

.        .        .        .        .        .

I often, often, think of our little ones that are
in the upper fold.  O some day, some day, we shall
meet and know them; and they shall not be ignorant
of us; and our hearts shall rejoice, and our joy no one
shall take from us.

With tender love,

D. A.

To the same:

I know the present suspense must tell heavily upon you; yet I am unable to give you further definite information to-day. I expect to have further advice to-day; but not in time for the mail. Yet, dear, He who has given you patience and strength, thus far, will not fail you now, nor in coming days. I can assure you that the days are passing quietly with me; and I have not any trouble about what may be to come. I long to live and labor; I long to live for and with you and the little ones; and it may be God's good pleasure to grant this.

Do not fear the thought of the operation. I am not troubled by it. It may be a means to some recovery of power.

How are the dear little ones? Are they still holding by their Christian hope? Dear little children, may they, from this time forth, ever be disciples of Jesus.

Friends here have been very kind to me. Mr. Williams, whom you met in Toronto, comes frequently to see me and brings me interesting reading matter. His sister-in-law has called on me twice. His mother, an elderly woman, is unable to come to see me, but has felt drawn to make my case one of special prayer. Others here have done and are doing the same. How much there is to be thankful for in this!

Now, dear, let courage and patience have their perfect work. Do not fear. Love to you all.

Yours,    D. A.

TO THE SAME:

.   .   ,   .   .   .   .   .   .

Your letter which reached me Saturday night, has done me much good.   .   .   .   We will trust God. He cannot err, and it may be that in His mercy happy days on earth are before us.   .   .   .

D. A.

---

TO THE SAME:

.   .   .   .   .   .

Your letter of last night has been very helpful to me.   You spoke of a feeling akin to assurance regarding my return to you, and you wrote that you could not want anything contrary to His will.   Now His will may be along the line of the assurance, for He hears prayer.   If His will should be otherwise, that will would still be best. Yet I think we are right in hoping and praying for recovery.   .   .   .   .   .   . .   .   .   .   .   Do not fear and do not be discouraged. I know you will hope in God, and I know He will not put your hope to shame.   .   .   .   .   God's peace be with you and with the little ones.

.   .   .   .   .   .   .

D. A.

---

TO THE SAME:

Another day of this strange school-life has passed for you and for me.   O what are the lessons He would have us learn and what is His purpose with regard to the future of our lives?   We don't know, we can't know what is to be the future for physical life and health. But we do know that He, who spared not his own Son when our interests required His sacrifice, is not bringing to bear upon us purposeless pain. The sufferings of this present time —and yours are not less than mine—have something to do in working out that which we are called to, and I think it must be through the change which discipline effects in life.

I feel glad to think of the little ones as interested in spiritual things. O may the unseen verities be not less real to them as the years pass by.

I think that I may ask you to pay me a visit, ere many weeks go by, for I think that I shall not very long delay the surgical operation, and I shall be glad to see you and talk with you before I take the step which I think will be necessary and which I think my case fully justifies. However, nothing will be done in a hurry; and please cast this with every other burden on Him who careth for us.

Now, dear Gussie, I am conscious of your love and of the love of the little ones; and I know that this enforced absence has told me how much my wife and little ones are to me.

With tender love to you all, and to Louise,

I am your husband,

D. A.

To the same:

Another day, and another letter, without anything very new to write. Yet the days as they

go by must bring some kind of change, and perhaps
that cannot be better expressed than Gertie has done
it, " If he doesn't get better he'll come back, and he'll
come if he does."         .      .      .      .      .      .

.      .      .      .   I had a letter from Prof. Wells last
evening.  He is such a busy man that I did not expect to hear from him, but his company has always
been so pleasant and profitable to me, that I was
specially glad when I noticed that the letter was from
him.      .      .      .      .      .      .      .      .
Be strong and of good courage.  I cannot forecast the
future, but if God be with us we can be courageous in
the dark.      .      .      .      .      .      .      .

D. A.

_____

To the same:

.      .      .      .      .      .      .
.      .      .   The retrospect for me is far from
gratifying.  In some few things, I think my heart
does not condemn me, but I would rejoice in recovery,
if so be that I might redeem the time.  Still, I have
decided not to mourn always over past failures, but
to strive to find rest and comfort in the truth that
salvation is all of *grace* and not at all of *works*.

.      .      .      .      .      .      .

D. A.

_____

To the same:

.      .      .      .      .      .   May He who
is able, under all circumstances, to give peace and
gladness, make the little home evermore a place of

quiet joy. . . . . . .

Dear little ones, how the heart longs for them and for you all—but patience must have her perfect work. .

. . . . . .

D. A.

---

MY DEAR LITTLE GERTIE:

Papa has been thinking about you and pray-ing to Jesus for you every day. I hope that you will soon be quite well again. Mamma wrote to me that you are trying to be a good little girl and it has made me glad. How glad I would be to-day to take you in my arms and kiss you. Well perhaps Jesus will make me well enough and keep you well enough that this may be some day. We will pray to Him for this. Will you and Edith kiss mamma and auntie and dear little baby for me ? And will my little Gertie trust and love and serve Jesus day by day?

My little darling, good-bye, in hope to see you some day.

Lovingly, PAPA.

---

DEAR FOLKS AT HOME:

Just a few lines to-day. I am not without hopes that I may see you again; but in case I may not, I would like to drop this note and say, good-bye. Gussie is with me and will stay till the crisis is over. She is calm and brave. She is a dear little woman, full of courage and tenderness. You will know ere this reaches you that the operation is to take place on

Friday afternoon; and probably that time will have arrived ere this reaches you. What results may follow, it is impossible to foretell. It may bring back a measure of power; it may leave me as I am; and there is a possibility that it may end life. I trust that in any event all is well. It will be pleasant, very pleasant, if I may be permitted to see you all again in this life. I would like much, too, to see the little ones at home. God will do what is best. I will see that Malcolm will let you know at an early date what the result of the operation is, so far as result can be told soon after the operation.

Much love to you, father, Maggie, Crissie and children.

Good-bye for a little while, I know not for how long; but I hope to see you yet in the flesh.

Very affectionately,

D. A

---

McMASTER HALL, TORONTO,<br>Dec. 11th, 1889.

MY OWN TWIN BROTHER:

It is coming near the 13th, and for this reason I write you.

.     .     .     .     .     .

Some months ago I did not expect to write you again on the anniversary of our birth. I therefore write to-day with a feeling of tenderness that is deeper than it otherwise could be. My dear Robert, with a heart that makes my eyes run over, I write to you to-day. The God who has blessed and prospered you thus far multiply His favors still more in days and years to come. May you have a happy, happy 13th, and let it not be clouded by the thought that I am lying here in comparative helplessness; but rejoice with me that God has been pleased thus far to spare my life to loved ones here and to loved ones with you. I desire to live, even though I may be encompassed with great infirmity. I think it will be better for my family; I think it will spare them a great sorrow; and I can be glad in the possibility of some service to do here on the earth. I cannot well endure the thought of being called away now, as I look on life with its poor and meagre service. Pray God, with me, that I may, as I hope, be spared to do work on earth for years to come.

.     .     .     .     .     .

Shall we both see another 13th of December here on earth? I know not. God knows. Whether this may be or not, may we spend a blessed eternity, hand in hand, on high. God gather all our loved ones into that blessed home, and may we have fellowship with Him and with them evermore.

With a heart of love,<br>Your twin Brother,<br>D. A. McGREGOR.

---

MY DEAREST BROTHER:

.     .     .     .     .     .

I think if there is any hope for me, that hope lies in the operation, humanly speaking. I know that much prayer has been offered to God for me, yet I know not what His will is, save that it is the outcome of His wisdom and love. To Him I resign wife and little ones, and my own life. Yet I pray for recovery if I may thereby accomplish not less by living than by dying.

.    .    .    .    .    .

Affectionately, your Brother,

D. A. McG.

———

MY DEAR ROBERT:

Just a little note to you to day.

.    .    .    .    .    .

I know, dear Robert, that I am about to undergo a very serious operation. . . . . God may bring me safely through it, and it may be the means to the recovery of some strength. I know, too, that in it I may end life. Yet my condition is such that I think it right for me to accept the risk. If I can I will write you again ere the operation takes place. If I should not, this may be my last letter to you. I trust that all is well, if life for me should soon end. I love you, Robert, as we have always loved each other; and in that love I embrace yours as well as you. Good-bye, dear Robert. I hope to see you on earth again, yet I know there is the other possibility.

With fond love, farewell,

Your Brother,

D. A.

Early in March it became evident that the surgical operation could not with safety be much longer delayed. As some time before this Dr. Weir had been called suddenly away to Europe, it was resolved, in accordance with his instructions, should necessity occur, to proceed at once with the operation without waiting for him. Fortunately his partner, Dr. Abbe, an expert of large experience and of the highest standing in spinal surgery, had now returned, after six months' absence, to his post as surgeon in St. Luke's Hospital. He was asked to take the case. After repeated examinations, to determine more fully the advisability of operating, the patient was removed to St. Luke's to be directly under Dr. Abbe's care. His loving and beloved wife was sent for, and she was thus enabled, for the last six weeks of his life, to the great comfort of them both, to be daily at his bedside. After quickly building up the patient's strength to prepare him for the ordeal, his physician set a time for the operation; but a violent attack of kidney and bladder complaint supervening compelled postponement and once more very nearly ended his life; and a little later, the same disappointing and perilous experience was repeated. But after several weeks of delay, thus rendered compulsory, the patient was found to be in a condition suitable for the operation; and, accordingly, the afternoon of Wednesday, the 16th of April, was chosen for the purpose. Dr. Weir had in the meantime returned, and generously arranged to be present to counsel and assist. It was no ordinary comfort and satisfaction to the sufferer, that these two

of the brightest lights in spinal surgery were together
to do their utmost to save his life and bring him back
to health ; and he regarded it as ground for the profoundest gratitude that without remuneration they
should, at such cost of valuable time and earnest
thought, and in so benevolent and kind a manner,
render him such important and responsible services
as scarcely any money could adequately repay.

With assured trust in his Saviour, and with a courage at once calm and cheerful, the patient gave himself up to the critical undertaking.   He was borne to
the operating table, etherized to unconsciousness, and
laid on his face on the operating table.   Dr. Abbe,
after giving to the assembly of physicians present a
brief history of the case, stated that, with Drs. Seguin
and Weir, he believed it to be a case of Pott's disease;
and that he expected to find the spinal bones in the
neighborhood of the eighth dorsal (a point midway
between the shoulder-blades), partly degenerated
through tubercular disease, and to find also inside of
the eighth dorsal, a tubercular tumor, whose pressure
upon the spinal cord was the cause of the paralysis.
With the utmost swiftness and precision, he then pro-
ceeded to cut into the spine, with various keen blades,
some of which had powerful leverage, a trench about
five inches long and three inches deep, and to remove
such parts of the bones as he found to be diseased.
Laying bare nearly three inches of the spinal cord,
he pointed out to those who were about him, a tough
and purplish tubercular tumor, which had grown out
of the diseased bones, and by its direct pressure on

the cord had caused the paralysis. On removal, the tumor was found to be in bulk nearly the size of a hen's egg; but the spinal cord itself was believed to be free from disease; and from this it was inferred with considerable confidence that recovery might be looked for. The wound was quickly filled in with antiseptic gauze, and left unsewed in order that it might be properly dressed from time to time, and to permit the healing process to be a healthy growth from within; and within an hour from the first pass of the knife, he was lying quietly in his bed in the ward.

For several hours during the night that followed, the invalid was in much peril from the shock; but in the morning he rallied, and his convalescence was so rapid and steady that on Saturday he had regained much strength, was in much physical and mental comfort, and was able easily to converse with his wife and brother. But on Sunday, though his strength was still increasing and his spirit was cheerful as a lark, a very slight hiccough set in; which, at the time, appeared to be too insignificant a matter to occasion apprehension. It continued, however, and increased day after day, being incited and maintained by severe stomachic disturbance and by a fresh and serious attack of kidney disorder; so that, by Friday morning, it absolutely wore him out, in spite of all that medical science could do.

During the greater part of the last night of his life, he was in profound slumber medically induced. But in the earlier part of the night before the soporific

took effect, and toward morning when its force was
spent, his eldest brother prayed and conversed with
him, briefly, several times; and always found him
clinging confidingly to his Saviour. When the petition was offered that the suffer might have "quiet-
ness and rest" (for whether awake or asleep, the ex-
hausting convulsive sob of the hiccough went steadily
on), he took up the phrase and repeated it like a re-
frain, and rang the changes on it, like a chime, till he
fell asleep, when, for the first time, the hiccough stop-
ped for a while. But, as the event proved, the hiccough was becoming feebler simply because the vital
forces were nearly spent.

When the morning was well advanced, his brother,
desiring to apprise him that, in all probability, death
was close at hand, asked him a question, which began
the following series of questions and replies, " Daniel,
do you believe in the Lord Jesus Christ with all your
heart ?" " Yes, I believe in the Lord Jesus Christ.
But does your question mean that the end of life has
come for me ?" " Yes, I fear that the end is very
near." " Do you mean to say that there is *absolutely*
no hope ?" " No, I do not say there is absolutely no
hope; for while you continue to breathe and the hiccough no longer is present, there is, apparently, a very
slight chance that you may recover. But I fear that
you have only a few hours to live." He seemed then
to be expressing to himself, in indistinct soliloquy, his
surprise at the result, and at the same time his soul's
trust in his Saviour. When the house-surgeon suggested that, if he could only get to sleep, he might

possibly rally, even yet, the sick and dying man turned his head upon his pillow and instantly went to sleep. When he wakened, which was not long afterwards, he appeared to be quietly resting; but soon he suddenly flung back his arms, gave one deep inspiration, and he was gone : for, though two physicians, who were present, instantly injected under the skin the most powerful stimulants, the heart refused to beat another stroke. Thus, at about eleven in the morning of Friday, April 25th, 1890, after a long and brave struggle with complicated and powerful disease, his ransomed spirit passed away from earth into the life and light beyond.

That evening his body, accompanied by his now widowed wife and his eldest brother, was on its way to Toronto. Over the scene of grief and desolation, upon its arrival in the now shattered home, we must draw a veil.

On Monday, April 28th, after a most devout, solemn and tender funeral service, in which many valued friends of the departed participated, and present at which a deeply sympathizing and sorrowing company filled the hall of the College, where the deceased Principal, but recently appointed, had earnestly hoped to do long and efficient service for Christ and His people, his earthly remains were borne to the not distant Mount Pleasant Cemetery, where the dust of his two departed children was lying, and committed to the ground "till the heavens shall be no more."

Of the mystery of the Divine procedure, in preparing a man through long and trying processes and

8

setting him apart for an important work, and then
almost immediately laying him aside by fell disease ;
in putting it into the hearts of the people of God to
pray, with unwonted unanimity and earnestness, for
his recovery and continuance in service, and then disappointing their profoundest desires and hopes ; in
granting, eventually, to his physicians, marked success
in removing the great primary cause of his physical
ailments, and in bringing him into encouraging convalescence, and then baffling their utmost efforts to
overcome a merely incidental complaint, it can only
be said, that it lies hidden in the sovereign and infinitely wise and holy counsels of Him whose "way is
in the sea," whose "path is in the great waters," and
whose "footsteps are not known." The vastness of
the Divine plans, comprehensive alike of all time and
of all space, the invincible limitations of the human
mind, and the deliberate purpose of God, in certain
things, to conceal Himself, preclude the possibility of
our comprehending many things which we would
greatly desire to understand. To employ certain
peculiarly significant words of Holy Writ, which were
oft-repeated as a watchword, on the lips, and potent
as a spell, in the heart of the departed, this mystery
must remain sealed till

"THE DAY SHALL DECLARE IT."

# CHAPTER VI.

## TRIBUTES OF RESPECT.

The following announcement of Principal McGregor's death and account of the funeral services are taken from the *Canadian Baptist:*

"The blow has fallen. The fond hopes of a host of loving friends have been disappointed and the gravest fears realized. The beloved Principal of our Theological College is dead. The letter from his brother in our last, giving a clear and graphic account of the surgical operation, its success in locating and removing the tumor which was the immediate cause of the disease, and the cheering prognostications of the attendant surgeons, enabled us to say that we awaited further tidings with hopeful anxiety. For a few days the telegrams continued to bring the most cheering accounts of progress. Then change for the worse came. The painful disease which had twice since his entrance into the hospital brought him to the very gates of death, again attacked him, with fatal results. All that medical skill could do to avert the issue was done, but in vain. On Thursday came the ominous message 'Prepare for the worst,' and on Friday the news that he who had for the past nine months been the object of so much loving and prayerful solicitude had peacefully gone to the eternal rest."

--------

"The earthly remains of the late Principal McGregor were laid in Mt. Pleasant Cemetery on Monday afternoon.   A solemn and impressive service was held at McMaster Hall, commencing at 3 p.m.   Rev. Dr. Welton, Acting Principal of the Theological Department, presided.   After an invocation by Rev. R. G. Boville and singing, a portion of Scripture was read by Rev. Dr. MacVicar, Chancellor of the University. Prayer was offered by Rev. Dr. Thomas, of Jarvis St. Brief addresses were then delivered by Rev. Messrs. John McLaurin, E. W. Dadson, Thomas Trotter, and Elmore Harris, acquaintances of long standing and intimate friends of the deceased.

"Rev. Mr. McLaurin said that he had known Mr. McGregor from early childhood, they having been born and brought up on adjacent farms, and having been members of the same church after their conversion and baptism.   The influences of those early days had never passed away.   Afterwards Mr. McGregor went to College, while he went to the far East as a missionary.   The early intimacy was renewed in 1886, when Mr. McGregor wrote to him in India, expressing his desire to give himself to missionary work and asking his advice.   Believing that his scholarly abilities would enable him to be more useful in his own land, Mr. McLaurin urged him to remain in Canada.

He loved the departed because the latter had believed in and loved his native land; had believed in and loved the young men of Canada and had dedicated his life to them.  Mr. McGregor's theological views were conservative.  He thought Christ and his apostles knew all about the nineteenth century, and its discoveries and wants, and were safe guides to follow.  He was gentle, genial, generous, clear-headed, warm-hearted, manly.  There was an exuberance of love in his character.  He was incapable of a mean or ignoble action.  May God give Canada many such men.

"Rev. Mr. Dadson knew that anything that he might say in praise of the departed would find an echo in every heart.  He had been pondering on the mysterious providences of God, as he remembered the number of men holding leading positions in the denomination that had been cut down in the prime of life.  Dr. Fyfe had been taken away, Professors Yule and Torrance had been taken, and now Principal McGregor.  The lesson was brought home with tremendous power that God can do without individual men, however useful or indispensable they may appear to be.  His work will go on, whoever falls.  They had, perhaps, depended too much on men instead of on God.  If this work of Christian education is to be well done, it must be through the power of God.  When Christ departed this life he commissioned his disciples to carry on his work.  He appealed to the teachers and students and to the Baptist people not to let the work in which Mr. McGregor had fallen flag, or cease to progress.

" Rev. Mr. Trotter felt that it would not be fitting to
use extravagant eulogy, but he wished to speak of
what he knew of their departed friend.  Mr. McGregor was not a perfect man, but he knew few things
that could be justly said about the greatest and best
men that could not justly be said about their brother.
He said this after an intimate acquaintance of over
eighteen years.  He referred to Mr. McGregor's intellectual endowments.  These gave him a high place at
College and University, made him a man strong in
the faith, a noble vicar of Christ, an able Professor in
the College, and finally Principal.  His great conscien-
tiousness led D. A. McGregor to desire above all things
to know the right, and nothing could deter him from
following what he believed to be right.  He was a
Christian man.  One ideal was ever before him, one
impulse urged him on, one life he wished to live.  The
strength of his convictions was great.  Though he had
probably accepted the Christian faith traditionally, he
had verified it by deep thought and personal experience.  Simplicity and modesty were native to him.
There was an entire absence of self-seeking in his
course.  As a friend he loved intensely, and was loved
intensely in return.  What he had accomplished had
been accomplished in comparative youth.  Had his
life been spared he must have fulfilled its great promise.

" Rev. Mr. Harris said that in the death of Mr. Mc-
Gregor he had lost a wise counsellor and a dear friend.
He spoke feelingly of the part the deceased had taken
in connection with the establishment of the Walmer

Road church. The death of Mr. McGregor left a great blank in his life. Did he not remember that this life is but a preparation for eternity, he would be utterly unable to comprehend such a bereavement. He believed their brother was now before the throne. His thoughts were full of the resurrection, while their hearts were full of grief. There was also room for Christian exultation, and they might well exclaim, "O grave, where is thy victory?" Mr. Harris, in closing, referred touchingly to the widow and children of the departed, in their overwhelming sorrow.

"After the singing of another hymn and prayer by Rev. J. Alexander, the casket was borne to the hearse by the pall-bearers, Professor Newman, Professor Campbell, Rev. E. W. Dadson, Rev. Thomas Trotter, Rev. Ira Smith, Rev. J. J. Baker, Rev. S. S. Bates, and Principal Huston. The remains were followed to Mount Pleasant Cemetery by the brothers, Rev. Malcolm MacGregor, of New York, and Mr. Robert McGregor, of Ottawa, by Mr. Hull, of Princeton, father-in-law, Rev. Mr. Corkery, of Wisconsin, and young Mr. Hull, brothers-in-law of the deceased, as chief mourners, and by a large number of sympathizing friends, including the forty students of the College. Prayer at the grave was offered by the Rev. W. K. Anderson, a former pastor of the deceased."

———

After giving an appreciative sketch of Principal McGregor's life, the Editor of the *Canadian Baptist* proceeds to give his own estimate of the character of the deceased, based on an intimate acquaintance of several years' duration.

"The writer had the happiness of knowing Mr. McGregor long and intimately, during the eight years of his student-life at Woodstock, and during three years since his appointment to a professorship in McMaster Hall, and could say much, most conscientiously and sincerely, in his praise. This would be superfluous in view of the testimony of several of those who were his fellow-students and most intimate College friends, which will be found in another column. Their words of eulogy are strong. We have seldom read or listened to the words of admiring and loving friends, uttered in praise of one just taken from them, without fearing that there was more or less tendency to exaggeration and extravagance. We can honestly say, on this occasion, that we have not that feeling in any appreciable degree. We feel that the words of affectionate eulogy are at the same time the words of truth. Take him all in all, we have never known a better balanced or more estimable character, or one in which we thought we could discern surer promise of future usefulness of no common order, than that of the deceased. It often happens, is in fact almost a rule, that superior mental endowments are to a greater or less extent marred by defects on the social or moral side of the character, and *vice versa*. The man of superior intellect is often irascible, reserved, or domineering; the man marked by special amiability frequently lacks mental acumen, or intellectual force.

The beauty of Mr. McGregor's character was its symmetry. Without being exactly brilliant he was one of the clearest thinkers, as student and as teacher, whom it has been our privilege to know. With a most loving and lovable nature were combined great strength both of intellect and of will. While constitutionally disposed, as his friend Mr. McLaurin observed, to be conservative in his theological views, his conservatism was not of that narrow kind which maintains itself by persistently looking on one side of questions, and reading one school of writers.

"During the early months of his illness, his mind seemed at times to be almost abnormally active. We sat sometimes by his bedside and discussed the hard problems of the age, until we felt it necessary repeatedly to ask him to desist, or to break off our visit abruptly, lest his mental activity should prove too much for his physical strength. Those earnest talks revealed a depth and intensity in that quiet nature which a cursory acquaintance would scarcely have suggested. Two complementary yet contrasted phases of this inner nature were delightfully brought to view. One was his earnest desire to know truth as truth, to have as clear conceptions of it as possible, in its metaphysical and theological aspects. The other was his earnest desire, too often not sufficiently associated with the former, to understand and use that truth in its practical applications to the needs, physical and social, as well as moral and religious, of suffering humanity. The condition of the masses, their poverty, hardships and temptations, the struggle between labor and capi-

tal,—such questions as these he was coming more and
more to see were most intimately related to the Christian life and the work of the Gospel ministry. His mind
was earnestly occupied, amongst other things, with a
plan for a series of lectures for the students in which
the relations of the preacher of the Gospel to these and
kindred problems of the age were to have been discussed.

"It was one of the rare excellencies of our departed
brother's character, that it was not necessary always
to agree with him in order to retain his cordial friendship. Like most strong characters he was tenacious of
his own opinions, and we sometimes differed both on
mere speculative points and in regard to such practical
questions as the best mode of organizing and carrying
on our educational work, and the proper relations of
its different departments. But no such differences,
however frankly discussed, ever produced the slightest
manifestation of ruffled feeling, or interfered in the
least with a warmth of friendship and affection which
will be among the most cherished recollections of a
lifetime. Long intercourse, first as teacher and student,
and afterwards as friends and neighbors, will, we trust,
excuse the personal tone of these reminiscences.

"On the religious side of our departed friend's spirit
and life we need not dwell. His devout piety was
well known by all who knew the man, for it was
a part of his very life. To one fact we may refer. His
burning desire to live and work for the Master in his
chosen sphere was remarkable. To the last it never
waned. He did not weary of the struggle as many
do, and in his sense of weakness long for the coming

rest. Above all and always he desired to live and work, to develop to the utmost the powers God had given him, and to consecrate them more fully in years of loving service. And yet there was no murmuring at the lot which decreed otherwise. Blended with all his strong desire was a will submissive, meek, resigned to the good and perfect will of the Master. This feeling was well expressed in the words of his favorite hymn,—Faber's: "I worship Thee, sweet will of God." He believed with perfect trust that—

'He always wins who sides with God,
 To him no chance is lost ;
God's will is sweetest to him when
 It triumphs at his cost.' "

In many of our churches in Toronto and throughout the Province reference was made to the great denominational loss, and a number of memorial sermons were preached. It would be impracticable to reproduce any of these in full, even if they were available. We limit ourselves to a newspaper report of the sermon preached by Rev. B. D. Thomas, D.D., in the Jarvis St. church :

"Know ye not that there is a prince fallen this day in Israel?"

"I have chosen these words for my text this evening in view of the event which has bowed the hearts of our whole Baptist Israel in this Province with sorrow. Daniel Arthur McGregor, so recently appointed Principal of McMaster Hall, and who was recognized throughout the denomination as one of the choicest spirits in our ministry, has, after many weary months of patient suffering, passed into the unseen. No event that has

occurred in years has touched our sensibilites more
keenly. The circumstances connected with it have
been such as to make it thrillingly pathetic. He was
a man in the very prime of his manhood. He had
been chosen to a high responsibility. He possessed
rare qualities of both head and heart, which he had
hoped to consecrate to the accomplishment of the
work entrusted to his hands. He had the confidence
of his brethren in a marked degree. The efficiency
which he exhibited as a professor in one of the departments of McMaster Hall, led to his appointment to the
Principalship on the resignation of Dr. Castle. Scarcely
had he entered upon this enlarged sphere of usefulness
and possibilities, when he was stricken down. At the
moment when life was opening out before him with
radiant promise, the fatal symptoms appeared. Is it
a strange thing that we should stand beneath the
shadow of such a Providence with mournful hearts?
Could it be otherwise? While love burns with fervent glow within our souls; while noble qualities
command veneration and esteem; while sympathy
with the aspirations of ability and worth abide; while
hearts beat warm to all that is high and noble, there
must be sorrow, in view of the swift ending of this
life so rare and promiseful.

"There is an aspect of this event which it would be
vain on mere philosophical principles to seek to understand. Looked at with a mere human vision, it is
inexplicable. It is a profound enigma, the elucidation
of which can come to us from no earthly sense. Why
all those years of unflagging industry, of great enthusi-

asm, of earnest preparation for high and grand achievements, to culminate in irrevocable disappointment? Why all this blossoming of exuberant nature to undergo a cruel blight, as the fruit was only ripening? Why all these rare qualities of intellect and heart to be buried in an untimely sepulchre? To stand in the presence of such a spectacle without a clear apprehension of the infinite purpose of life, would be sad indeed. But we sorrow not as 'those without hope. We are sustained and comforted with the conviction that it is not all of life to live nor all of death to die. When we shall have spent the years we are to live, we are embraced in the infinite plan of eternity. What we mourn over to-day is not a failure, but a change leading to a higher fruition and development. What is to us a sad ending, is to him for whom we mourn a loftier beginning. Nothing has been lost. The very weariness and pain have been beneficent ministrations in the unfolding of the Divine purpose. All the years of toil and study have entered into the nature of his soul with a beneficent and purposeful intent.

" The speaker then applied the words of the text to the deceased man, pointing out that, as an earnest Christian, he was of royal birth — a prince to be honored. He had a royal nature. He had a royal education. He had a royal sphere. He had a royal fellowship. He has a royal crown. We should be thankful that God gave us such a life. Its sweet purity and guilelessness, its manly earnestness and fidelity, its quiet strength and fascinating sweetness will long abide with us as a rich legacy of blessing.

Let them all strive so to live, that, when their own time came to pass away to the unseen, they might be as ready to depart as was D. A. McGregor. He was a prince who had fallen, and for him there awaited a crown of glory which would never fade."

---

From the *Woodstock College Monthly* we copy the following editorial notice :

" He has gone. Many sad hearts are feeling more and more their sorrow and realizing more and more their loss. The life of D. A. McGregor was so strongly calm and peaceful that even in his death his influence is felt in the nature of the sorrow it has created. There is on all hands a deep abiding sorrow, full of anguish, and yet tempered and controlled by a deep abiding peace, full of glory. In death as in life our brother was a peace-maker; in these last sad days his character has received another crown of praise in that it has governed and channelled our sorrow.

" Principal McGregor will be missed. Toronto Baptist College will miss him. He was ever true to the interests of ministerial education, of which he had a high ideal. His place as a leader may be supplied— some of the qualities of originality, of foreseeing and providing, he may not have possessed to the highest degree—but as a strong teacher, and as a friend of ministerial students, as a clear-headed dispassionate adviser, as firm and yet gentle, soothing and yet persuasive, he was alone.

" The churches will miss him. ' Blessed are the peace-
makers for they shall be called the children of God.'
D. A. McGregor was essentially a peace-maker. He
never stirred up strife and bitterness. Never afraid
nor slow to state his views, he was aways temperate
and never harsh, always considerate, always sincere.
How often have his words thrown a spell of peace
over our agitated meetings, and caused bitterness to
melt away into rivers of love. Surely the churches
may exclaim.

> ' *When comes such another.*'

"The Home and Foreign Missions will miss him.
His heart was filled with sympathy for every enterprise that had for its object the good of the world, in
the upbuilding and saving of souls. His influence as
Secretary of the Home Mission Society will not die.

" Woodstock College will miss him. The College
interests are mentioned last because they are dearest
to our hearts. We at Woodstock do indeed already
miss our brother. He did not live with us. He was
associated with another branch of our educational
work, but he was for us. His sympathy was a power
to us all. To some of the masters he had been a college companion, to none of them was he unknown,
and to none of them had he failed to give strength
by his quiet indication of sympathy and of fidelity to
the college cause. The college flag that hung at half-
mast, the college bell that tolled its mournful notes at
the hour appointed for the funeral, the deputation
that represented the college at that funeral, meant

more than merely the death of an old boy; they represented the sadness and sorrow that come to those that
realize that they have lost a portion of themselves.
We are not what we were. We have, in the times
that are gone, been encouraged by his interest and
cheered by his counsel ; we felt him to be one of ourselves.   He is gone.

"And yet his strong life still lives.   He is not dead.
Apart altogether from existence in a land of purer
delight, in a home of greater possibilities, he is still
living.   His example, his memory, his character, his
own self, are with us, and we move forward inspired
by the thought that comes from the backward look
upon his life.

> ' We were weary, and we
> Fearful, and in our march
> Fain to drop down and to die.
> Still thou turnedst, and still
> Beckonedst the trembler, and still
> Gavest the weary thy hand.
> If in the paths of the world,
> Stones might have wounded thy feet,
> Toil or dejection have tried
> Thy spirit, of that we saw
> Nothing ; to us thou wast still
> Cheerful, and helpful, and firm ;
> Therefore to thee it was given
> Many to save with thyself,
> And at the end of thy day,
> O faithful shepherd ! to come
> Bringing thy sheep in thy hand.' "

The *Messenger and Visitor*, whose honored editor
has succeeded Mr. McGregor in the chair of Systematic Theology and Apologetics. and who had known

him intimately at Woodstock, published the following notice :

"It is with a sad heart that we write these mournful words. As our Ontario correspondent writes, an operation was performed upon his spine. About three inches of the spinal cord were laid open by cutting through the backbone. A tumor nearly as large as an egg, which had been pressing upon the great nerve centre, was removed, and strong hopes were had that he would recover. On Saturday came the tidings that he was dead. In his death the world has lost one of its truest men, and the work of our denomination one of its strongest but most unassuming workers. Very many of us feel we have lost one of our best friends. It was our privilege to know him intimately as a student at Woodstock College, during the years of our ministry with the church there, and for few did we ever grow to have a greater respect or warmer love. His unaffected sincerity, his unswerving loyalty, his deep piety and devotion, all blended with a loving gentleness and modesty, formed a character of sterling worth and beauty. We cannot recall without emotion the last time we saw him. It was on our visit to Toronto last autumn. He was completely and cheerfully submissive to the divine will, while longing to have the privilege of continuing his work. He was much moved by the sympathy and good-will of his brethren. Before leaving he asked us to have worship with him. As we leaned over him to bid him good-bye, he drew us down, and we feel that the parting was indeed holy. As we turned at the door for a

9

last look, his eyes were fixed upon us with a wistful, intent gaze, prompted, we have no doubt, by the feeling that probably we should never meet again on earth. Is it any wonder that we shall always cherish the memory of that half-hour as most sacred?

"McMaster Hall has met with a very severe loss, and his growing power will be missed in all the work of our brethren in the west Already strong in mental and heart power, he had that humility which would ever have kept him striving to become better and stronger for his work.

"So the workmen fall: how comforting the thought that the work goes on, assured of triumph because raised above peradventure by Him who is all-powerful and all-wise."

---

The Senate and the Board of Governors of McMaster University passed the following resolution and sent a copy thereof to Mrs. McGregor:

"We, the Board of Governors and Senate of Mc-Master University, desire to take the earliest opportunity of expressing our deep sorrow at the death of Professor D. A. McGregor, B.A., late Principal of Toronto Baptist College. In our deceased brother and fellow-laborer we recognized a man of superior mental and spiritual endowments who by his many gifts and virtues commanded universal confidence and love. His work as a Professor was highly valued. In the Principalship of the College to which he had been so recently appointed we confidently hoped to see him achieve a great work for God. His early death, removing him from his great work almost before he had touched it, and cutting him off in the very prime of his manhood, has filled us with disappointment and sorrow. We bow submissively to the Divine appointment, but our sense of loss is very great. To Mrs. McGregor, who has been so sorely bereaved, and under such painful circumstances, we would tender our deepest sympathy, praying that the consolations of God may abound towards her, and that upon her and her dear children in all their future the special blessing of heaven may abide."

---

The students of McMaster Hall addressed the following letter of sympathy to Mrs. McGregor:

"The sad death of our dear Principal has stricken us with grief. During his brief connection with our College, we learned to esteem him for his talents, to honor him for his sterling worth, and to love him for his sympathy. A year ago when the Principalship became vacant, all eyes turned toward him and our hearts throbbed with joyful satisfaction when it was announced that he had been appointed to this position, for we knew how his heart yearned to help his brethren and the good his gentle influence would work in our lives. But he has been taken from us. No longer shall we listen to his voice nor feel his heart beat in sympathy with ours. The Lord has called him from

this life.    But he still lives in many lives and in them
he will influence multitudes for good.    Our loss is
great, our sorrow keen.    How heavy therefore must
your affliction be!    You have lost a loving husband,
your little ones are fatherless.    Kindly accept our
deepest sympathy in your sad loss.    We pray that
He who erreth not will comfort and sustain you by
his grace.    In love He has afflicted you.

> ' He chose this path for thee
> And well he knew that thou must tread alone
> Its gloomy vales and ford each flowing stream ;
> Knew how thy bleeding heart would, sobbing, moan,
> Dear Lord, to wake, and find it all a dream.
> Love scanned it all, yet still could say, ' I see
>         This path is best for thee.'"

From a large number of sympathetic letters addressed to the relatives of the deceased three have
been selected for reproduction here.    Rev. J. F. Elder,
D.D., and Rev. Leighton Williams, of New York,
whose letters addressed to Rev. Malcolm MacGregor
follow, knew Principal McGregor only as an invalid,
and showed him much kindness during his hospital
life :

" It was with deep sorrow that we learned last Sunday that our hopes and prayers for your brother's
recovery had not in God's good providence been answered according to our expectations. He has ordered
it otherwise, and we will believe that it is well, for
He doeth all things well—well for your brother—well
for his widow and children—well for the work from
which he is taken, and well for us all to whom he was

dear. Yea, doubtless, it is well, and far better if we could but see it, for our Father's ways are higher than our ways and His thoughts than our thoughts, and they are thoughts of inexpressible tenderness and infinite concern for our greatest blessedness. If there were no death, where would the glorious resurrection be? "He that loseth his life shall find it." Oh to realize this truth in the daily life, so that like Paul we 'die daily,' that the life also of Jesus might be manifest in our bodies. God bless and comfort you. II Kings iv: 26, and II Cor. 1: 3-7.

Affectionately yours,<br>LEIGHTON WILLIAMS."

" It made me feel very sad to see the announcement of your brother's death. I greatly enjoyed the few calls I made upon him and have seldom met one to whom I felt so drawn on brief acquaintance. His enthusiasm for his work, his patient submission to the will of God, and a certain undefinable charm of manner made him very engaging to me. My first visit gave me a sermon. He spoke freely and calmly of the terrible ordeal he was to pass through; and in reply to a suggestion of mine, that, even if the operation for his relief should result fatally, he would but be transferred to other service for his Lord, he said quickly and softly "I believe that: 'His servants shall serve Him.'"

"If we could but forget our own sense of loss, how

we could rejoice for him, called to service in the immediate presence of Christ—a service for which his very afflictions have been preparing him. Nor is his influence for Christ spent here below. Such a man lives on in those who have felt the charm of his presence and the inspiration of his enthusiasm.

"My heart goes out to the widow and orphans in their affliction. May he who is the Father of the fatherless and the widow's God make them to feel that the eternal God is their refuge and underneath are everlasting arms.

"May the God of *all* comfort give you adequate balm for your own wounded spirit: and may we both be the better servants of our Master for the example of him who was so lovely and pleasant in his life.

Yours truly,

J. F. ELDER."

We have purposely reserved till the last the tender, affectionate, beautifully written letter addressed by Dr. John H. Castle, himself rapidly approaching the end of earthly life, to Mrs. McGregor:

"Only this morning on opening the *Examiner* did I learn of your great sorrow in the death of my dear, dear friend, your beloved husband. I was expecting just as soon as his brother gave me the word that it was safe for him to converse with a friend to run over to New York and see him, and was looking forward to next week or the week following as the time when he would be sufficiently recovered from the shock of the operation to afford me the great privilege of another interview. But this was not to be, already he had gone 'to be with the Lord.' I had continued to pray for him a whole week after he had entered into his rest. I need not tell you how sincerely I loved and trusted him. He had my full confidence long before his connection with the College, and in the years we wrought together every day enhanced my affection for him as a sincere, self-denying, strong and faithful fellow-laborer. How little a year ago we could have anticipated the change which has occurred. No one would have been surprised, if I had gone 'the way of all the earth,' but he seemed strong and well, and just entering on a career of highest usefulness and honor. I remain, with health so much improved that I have been doing partial work in the ministry with unspeakable joy. He has finished his course. And yet to our view his life was so much more valuable than mine. But you know how firmly he believed that the inscrutable ways of God are holy and good. In the pure light of heaven he praises God for every step of the journey. It is now quite certain, I suppose, that he could only have survived a little while without the operation; so his friends cannot regret that he bravely faced the ordeal which promised possible recovery and usefulness. In your deep grief you have our warmest sympathy. We too have lost a precious friend whose memory is embalmed in recollections of love, purity, principle and Christlike action. Commending you to Him who sustains his children in their keenest sorrows, Mrs. Castle joins in mingling our grief with yours."

# PART II.

# LITERARY REMAINS.

# DOES POETRY NECESSARILY DECLINE WITH THE ADVANCE OF CIVILIZATION ?*

In Lord Macaulay's essay on Milton, we find the position taken, that, " As civilization advances, poetry almost necessarily declines "; and that superior mental culture, so far from being an advantage to the poet, is one of his greatest hindrances.   We know that he is not exceptional in the position he has taken ; for other writers of distinction, among whom is Lord Jeffrey, have maintained the same : yet we cannot but feel doubtful with regard to its correctness.   Lord Macaulay admits that his statement is rather paradoxical ; but he advances arguments to prove that it is nevertheless true.   He notices the facts that the poetical element of a nation's literature is the first to develop itself ; that it attains to a considerable degree of perfection while yet science is comparatively unknown ; and that science and philosophy are only developed in an enlightened age.   While the truth of these statements is evident to every reader of history, yet we fail to see that they afford any basis for the conclusion, that with the advancement of philosophy there will necessarily be a decline in poetry ; that " in an enlightened age there will be much science and philosophy, but little poetry ;" that "in proportion as

* From *The Tyro*, of April 1874.

men know more and think more, they will make better theories and worse poems." That philosophy does
advance with civilization, no one need doubt; but
does its advancement involve the decline of poetry?
We fail to see how the culture and refinement which
promote the one prove injurious, rather than beneficial, to the other. While we think that no one who
lacks the natural qualifications can become a true poet
by culture, we are not at all prepared to admit that a
thorough education and a high state of social refinement prove detrimental to the poetic art. On the
contrary, we think that the culture which is necessary to the full appreciation of true poetry, is also
necessary to its production. Every other occupation
advances with the civilization and higher education of
the people. Every other sphere of literary effort is
enriched by mental discipline. It is but natural to
expect that the growing efficiency of the power exercised should be followed by improvement in the work
performed; and we fail to see what there is in poetry
which causes it so to clash with Nature's universal
law. If that excellency of thought, purity of taste,
and power of expression, all of which are essential to
true poetry, are to be found in their highest perfection
in the ages of ignorance and barbarity, and decline as
civilization advances, what is mental culture? what is
social refinement? and what are their benefits? Yet
the statement that "the earliest poets are generally
the best," Lord Macaulay calls "the most orthodox
article of literary faith." One of the arguments which
the author uses in support of his position is, the effect

which the poetry of the early ages produced on the minds of the people. It is true that the wild effusions of a fiery brain in an age when superstition held the throne of reason, would rouse more terribly the minds of the people, than would any poem in an enlightened age. But are we to ascribe this to the perfection of the poetic art, or to the uncultivated taste of a people who knew no criterion of excellence but the wild agitation of feeling harrowed by scenes of horror ? The author might argue in the same manner, that because any commonplace distribution of glaring colors on canvas would produce livelier sensations in many an untrained mind, than would an exquisite picture in that of a skilled artist, therefore the ruder painting displays a higher perfection of the art. In the early stages of literature, the most extravagant outburst of an untrained imagination would, in all probability, be preferred to the well-wrought imagery and chaste expression of later times. So also would the common commingling of sounds in music be more appreciated by the untrained ear, than would the grander symphonies of Beethoven; yet a true judge of music would decide very differently with regard to their merit. In the same manner, though an uncultivated people might prefer the meaningless verses of a ballad-monger to the choicest stanzas of Tennyson, yet no person of good taste would come to the same conclusion ; and we cannot think that Lord Macaulay himself, though he places the golden age of poetry in the past, would exchange the choice thoughts and pleasing expressions of the poets of the last centuries for the vague productions of earlier times.

The author advances another argument and says, that "language, the machine of the poet, is best fitted for his purpose in its rudest state." If the rudeness of language only meant that rugged style which makes up in strength what it lacks in beauty, the argument would be one of force; but when we take into consideration that baldness and vulgarity, so characteristic of language in its earliest forms, and remember that on account of its poverty, the nicest shades of thought could never be expressed, we fail to see how he, whose themes are the most æsthetic, can find it the best adapted to his purposes.

The author again argues, that the progress of philosophy involves the decline of poetry, because the mode of thought necessary to the one is injurious to the other. This would probably be true in the case of a single individual, as no one can be truly successful in any one occupation who distributes his power among many; but when it is applied to a nation's progress, we think it proves faulty. It might as well be argued, that because agriculture is now carried on more efficiently and extensively than it was in the earlier ages, therefore there necessarily is a decline in the mercantile business, while, in reality, the one is the assistant of the other.

He also speaks of the very thorough education that Milton received—and it certainly was one of the first order—and then, from the position that literary proficiency is a hindrance to the highest attainments in poetry, he argues, that no poet has ever triumphed over greater difficulties than did Milton. If intellectual culture be detrimental to the poetic art, then almost all poets of distinction have had to contend with the same difficulty. How is it, then, that they so strangely burst the bonds of their fate and soared to eminence, while those who never had such difficulties to hinder their progress scarcely ever rose above the common level ? Arguing from the same standpoint, we would legitimately conclude, that the first attempts of a poet at metrical composition would be his most successful ; yet this would not agree with common experience and observation. Is it not more likely that the training which enables us to perceive the beauty of thought, would also cultivate the power of its conception and expression ? We fail to see how that discipline which quickens mental activity, gives breadth and energy of thought, grace and beauty of expression, can be a hindrance to him whose themes are the most æsthetic, and who therefore requires the rarest capabilities. We believe that there is much truth in the adage, " *Poeta nascitur non fit*," yet we as fully believe that England's poetry would never have sparkled so brightly on her literary page, had her poetic talent been unaided by thorough discipline. And we venture to say that, if it were not for that thorough culture, which Lord Macaulay calls a poet's hindrance, Milton's sublimest epics would lack that highest perfection which their able critic so much admires. We believe that a thorough education would prove a benefit to poetry, by ridding the world of much contemptible rhyme ; and while it might lessen, to a certain extent, the quantity of *lyric* poetry, yet, as a general rule, its

quality would be improved.   We think that both
poetry and philosophy will be found in their highest
degree of perfection in an enlightened age; and that
the thorough control over the intellectual faculties,
which severe discipline alone can secure, cannot fail
to have a beneficial influence on poetic productions.

---

## WHAT CONSTITUTES A REGULAR BAPTIST CHURCH ?*

If a Christian makes his choice of church connection
a matter of conscience toward God, and not simply one
of personal convenience, then a knowledge of what a
church is, in faith and practice, must precede his entrance into its fellowship.  If he unites with one body
of Christians rather than with another—if he invites
fellow-Christians to union with that body rather than
with another—the only worthy reason for his doing
so must be his conviction that the body with which
he is connected is a truly Scriptural Church.  But how
can he know this if he be not acquainted himself with
the accepted beliefs of the body with which he stands
identified ?   There must be some knowledge of church
belief or practice as a ground of preference between
different systems of church organization, else the up-
holding of one rather than another differs not from the
blindest partyism.   If churches are not to take their

---

*A paper read at the Ministerial Institute, in Jarvis St. Church,
1880.

scripturalness as a thing for granted, they must prove it by comparison with the Divine standard. But how can such comparison be instituted if there be not definite knowledge of the positions held ? Since correctness of faith and practice may be known only by comparison with Scripture—and since there cannot be comparison without a knowledge of the things to be compared—it cannot be unimportant to inquire into what constitutes a regular Baptist Church. As, by the wording of this question, I shall be brought to the frequent repetition of the term, "Regular Baptist Church," I wish to state that I use it not by way of ostentatious title. The name in itself is nothing. It is used simply as the briefest description of the particular organization now under discussion.

In stating the various elements which, in their combination, constitute a Regular Baptist Church, we mention first *the essential character of its membership.*

A Regular Baptist Church is a society of converted persons. Regeneration is not only a doctrinal belief, but an indispensable qualification for church fellowship. By this we do not mean that a church exercises an omniscience which guards it from all deception, but that none are received into its fellowship without first having given satisfactory evidence, so far as the church can judge, of personal salvation through faith in the Son of God. A Regular Baptist Church is not composed of believing parents and their children, but of believers, and believers only. Christian parentage gives no title to and no fitness for its fellowship. The question is not one of youth or age, of Christian cr un-Christian birth, but of a personal quickening from a state of spiritual death to life in Christ. The sons and daughters of the Lord God Almighty are not so by mere natural birth. There is no sonship in God's family, and no true membership in His church, apart from the reception of Christ. To as many as received Him, to them gave He power to become the sons of God, even to them that believe on His name, which were born not of blood, nor of the will of the flesh, nor of the will of man, but of God. A manifest desire to flee from the wrath to come is, in itself, no qualification for its membership. The church presents itself not as the sinner's refuge, but as the home of the saved. It is not the sphere in which conversion is to be wrought, but is itself the converted and converting agency which works under God for the salvation of the world. But if the church is thus to be, under God, the light of the world, its members cannot be the children of darkness. The living temple for God's indwelling cannot be composed of those who are dead in trespasses and sins. Believing, therefore, that the church of God is a spiritual body, a spiritual birth and a spiritual life are, in a Regular Baptist Church, made a condition and a characteristic of membership. This, and this alone, can satisfy the apostolic description of the churches of God : "Ye are all the children of God by faith in Christ Jesus ; for as many of you as have been baptized into Christ, have put on Christ." No body of Christians can, therefore, be acknowledged as a Regular Baptist Church, if it has not made a regenerated life a test question of membership.

But further. A Regular Baptist Church is composed not simply of those who are regenerated, but of those regenerate persons who have submitted themselves to Christian baptism, upon a profession of faith. By Christian baptism we mean the immersion of a believer in water, into the name of the Father, and of the Son, and of the Holy Ghost. If the act be any other than immersion, then it is not that which Christ instituted. If the person be any other than a believer, then he is not the person Christ designates. If the person be a believer, and the act be immersion, yet, if the baptism be not in the name of the Father, and of the Son, and of the Holy Ghost, it is not Christian baptism. It is not what Christ commanded to be done. The formula of Christian baptism is not less important than the act enjoined or the subject specified; and that is not Christian baptism which, in any way, either by change or omission, interferes with the Divine institution. Therefore no persons are scripturally baptized but those who, on a profession of faith, have been immersed in water, into the name of the Father, and of the Son, and of the Holy Ghost. This is not only Regular Baptist Church belief, but as Christ has placed baptism at the threshold of church relations, so none are received into Regular Baptist Churches but those who have thus submitted to His ordinance. Any church which administers any other rite in the name of baptism, or receives into its membership any others than those who are thus baptized, is not a Regular Baptist Church.

But more than this. Regeneration and baptism,

though indispensable prerequisites to church membership, do not in themselves constitute their subjects a
Regular Baptist Church. Men may be regenerated
and baptized, and yet be members of no visible church
whatever. They thus have fitness for membership,
but there can be no membership without organization.
A Regular Baptist Church is, therefore, an organized
body. It is not only an organized body, but a local
organization. The expressions, "Regular Baptist
Church," and "Regular Baptist Denomination," are
by no means synonymous. Though the words are
often used interchangeably, such usage embodies an
unscriptural assumption. The Regular Baptist denomination is not a church; nor is any denomination a
church. Denomination is nothing but a term which
distinguishes or designates various churches of the
same faith and order. A church of Christ on earth
in no sense comprises all those who hold similar views
of Gospel truth. The churches of Christ were many
in apostolic times, when there was a perfect unity of
belief. The churches of Christ are still many, as dis-
tinct local assemblies, and they can blend their identi-
ties in no other unity than that of the church invisible.
A Regular Baptist Church is, therefore, a local organization of baptized believers, associated by mutual
consent, in the faith, and love, and labor of the Gospel
—for the maintenance of the pure worship of God,
for the spread of His truth, and for the proper observance of His ordinances. Thus far, we have found the
essential elements which enter into the constitution of
a Regular Baptist Church to be a regenerated life and

a scriptural baptism, without which there cannot be proper subjects for church membership; and these subjects united in local organization, without which there cannot be church existence.

The second essential element, which we would mention as entering into the constitution of a Regular Baptist Church, is *the doctrinal basis of its unity.*

That a definite form of doctrinal belief is requisite to Regular Baptist Church existence, is seen from the simple fact that there are church organizations which are one with us in their beliefs concerning the ordinances, and who differ from us only on doctrinal grounds—and yet with them we have no church fellowship. If there were no doctrinal differences, the denominations would be one. If doctrinal belief were not a test question with Regular Baptist Churches, these differing denominations would still be one. The fact that they are not one, while doctrinal belief is the only difference, proves mainly that in Regular Baptist Churches doctrinal belief is regarded as an indispensable basis for church unity.

I cannot here state in full the teachings which, in a doctrinal point of view, characterize a church as one of Regular Baptist faith. This would be work not for a short address, but for a treatise on theology. Yet, perhaps, the briefest outline of that faith is here necessary.

The faith of Regular Baptist Churches, concerning God, is, that there is one, and only one, living and true God—the infinite, intelligent, eternal, self-existent Spirit—the first cause of all things—glorious in

His perfections, tri-personal in His existence, and yet, at the same time, essentially and eternally one.

Their beliefs concerning man are, that he is the creation of God. By the will of his Maker he is to remain a living, conscious being forever. His eternal blessedness, not his eternal existence, was conditioned upon his obedience. By sin, he involved himself and all his race in hopeless ruin, under the curse of law and the reign of death.

They believe that the Holy Scriptures, as originally given, are God's revelation to man, and are the infallible guide and supreme standard of all creeds and of all conduct.

The faith of a Regular Baptist Church, in reference to the law of God is, that it is that system of moral government under which man was placed in his creation, and under which he still lives. That same law, the unchanged standard of perfect life, was afterwards given to man in written record by the pen of inspiration. The law is holy, just, and good, and is incumbent upon all mankind. All its claims had to be satisfied before salvation could be offered to any of the human family ; therefore, all men must be, by nature, under its condemning power. Its penalties still rest on all who are not redeemed from its curse. Nor has Christ, in His vicarious work, in any way abrogated that law. It is by His fulfilment of law that he has brought his people out from under its condemnation. And He has brought them out from under its condemnation, not that it might be no longer their rule of life, but that the righteousness of the law might be fulfilled in us, who walk not after the flesh but after the Spirit.    But the righteousness of the law could not be fulfilled in us if it were not our rule of life. It is, therefore, in its unchanged perfection of holiness, justice and goodness, the glorious standard of all moral excellency, the abiding rule of all Christian life.    Do we then make void the law through faith ?    God forbid !   yea, we establish the law.

The faith that characterizes a Regular Baptist Church, in reference to the way of salvation, may be briefly designated as Pauline or Calvinistic.    By the election of grace, by the redemption of Christ, by the power of the Spirit, by belief of the truth, apart from any human merit, men are made new creatures in Christ Jesus, and preserved unto the day of His coming.

The Sabbath is believed to be an Edenic institution, and as such, it was designed for the whole human family, and for all time.    The Sabbath was made for man, and not simply for a small section of the human race.    It was given to man as needful for him even in his innocency.    How much more after his fall.    It is a divine institution which has never been abolished, and, therefore, carries with it perpetual obligation. The ceremonies connected with its observance by ancient Israel were exclusively national, and ceased with the abolition of the ceremonial law : but the original Sabbath, which, in its primitive simplicity, was not for the Jew only, but for man universally, could not perish in the dissolution of that which was merely national.    The Lord of the Sabbath saw fit to change the day of its observance, and to make it commemorative, not only of the works which were finished from the creation, but also of the completed redemption which crowned the resurrection morn. The first day of the week is, therefore, now observed, by His appointment, as the Lord's Day or Christian Sabbath. It is to be spent in freedom from secular toil, and in the special worship of God. Remember the Sabbath day to keep it holy.

In reference to the doctrine of last things, the faith of Regular Baptist Churches is, that, at the last day, Christ, the appointed judge of men, shall descend from heaven. The dead that are in their graves shall hear His voice, and come forth ; they that have done good unto the resurrection of life, and they that have done evil unto the resurrection of damnation. Christ will then give to all their final awards. The righteous will be adjudged to endless blessedness, and the wicked to equally endless misery. These shall go away into everlasting punishment, but the righteous into life eternal.

I have thus striven, with the greatest brevity I could command, to present the faith of a Regular Baptist Church, concerning God and man, law and gospel, present institutions, and final things. I am conscious of the very great imperfection of the presentation, but the time allotted to me will not permit me to do more.

It may be objected that a definite system of doctrine cannot be an essential element in the constitution of a Regular Baptist Church, since many persons

are members in our churches who are not able to pronounce definitely, even upon the few articles of faith
we have here enumerated. It is true that many, perhaps the majority, of those received into the fellowship of Baptist churches need clearer preception of
the things which are most surely believed among us
as a body. Yet this does not invalidate the statement
that a definite system of doctrine is an essential element in the constitution of Regular Baptist Churches.
In schools of instruction, there are those who, either
from inability or inapplication, fail to attain to a
knowledge of the principles which the schools seek to
inculcate. Yet this is far from proving that no such
principles are taught. The most positive and definite
system of truth may be propounded, and yet, some
may fail to apprehend it. The question, then, is not
to be decided on the ground of the pupil's want of
comprehension, but by an examination of the author-
ized system of instruction. So the question as to
whether a church has a definite form of doctrine, and
whether that form be regularly Baptistic, is not decided by the erroneous belief of a private member,
but by an examination of the teachings which the
church, as a body, accepts and sanctions. Churches
may thus have in them members who know not the
certainty of the things wherein they have been in-
structed, and yet be Regular Baptist Churches, but
they cannot teach different systems of doctrine, and
yet be said to have but one faith. If there were not
a oneness of faith, as a basis of church unity, then
church organization would be but a mockery of the

Most High. The Gospel is a positive system of truth, or it is nothing; and a church is a church of God's institution only in so far as it holds the doctrines and ordinances which the Gospel reveals and enjoins. A Gospel church has one faith as truly as it has one Lord and one baptism. Its unity is a unity of the faith. Its members are knit together in belief of the truth. If doctrinal belief were no condition for church membership, but simply professed attachment to the person of Christ, then might the doors of our churches be flung open to Unitarian, Universalist, Antinomian and Annihilationist, and the doctrine of devils might be accepted as the faith of God's elect. If Regular Baptist Churches can fellowship every form of doctrine under the sun, then they are no longer the churches of the living God. The church of the living God is a pillar and ground of truth. But a church cannot be at the same time the pillar and ground of truth and the home of heresy. If Regular Baptist Churches be the pillar and ground of truth, then they cannot be the careless introducers of false doctrine; and if they can lend their patronage to false doctrine, then they are no longer a pillar and ground of truth. But if they are not the pillar and ground of the truth, they are no longer the churches of the living God. And if they be not the churches of the living God, then what do we here in prayer and effort for their promotion? In our belief, then, at least, they must be the pillar and ground of the truth, else we sin in seeking their prosperity. But how can we esteem them to be the pillar and ground of the truth, if it be

true that doctrinal belief is no condition of membership ? If the declarations of faith of the Regular
Baptist Churches may read thus :—We do, and we do
not, believe the following doctrines; we teach this
definite system of truth, and we teach the contrary ;
we have one faith and one order, and yet can accom-
modate every variety of belief and lawlessness ; how
can such churches be the pillar and ground of the
truth ? If our faith is made up of such degenerate
folly, then Regular Baptist Churches are not the
churches of the living God. Let us then either resign
our high claims to be apostolic churches, or let us recognize the essentiality of our doctrinal beliefs to our
church existence.

Another characteristic of a Regular Baptist Church,
is *the nature and number of its permanent offices.*
Its distinctly official positions are two, the pastoral
and the diaconal. The church has power to elect persons to, or depose them from, these official positions,
but it has no power to change the offices themselves.
It may exist, as a church, under such circumstances,
that for a time, it may be without fit persons to fill
the vacant offices, and yet, so long as the offices themselves are recognized, the church is, in this respect,
Regular. But the moment it interferes with these
divine appointments by discarding any of the offices
as unnecessary, or by substituting for them any other
system of management, that moment it ceases to be a
Regular Baptist Church. It has violated God's institution. I shall make no further statement in reference to this position, as the thought is to be elabo-
rated in another address.

Another factor, essential to Regular Baptist Church existence, is *its form of government*, which is that of congregational independency. Free from State aid and State legislation, it leans not on the arm of political power. Within itself it submits to no hierarchical or episcopal supremacy. It is under the legislative authority of no organized body on earth, whether Conference, Presbytery, Association or Union, but believes the laws of Christ to be all-sufficient for its guidance apart from all human interference. Each church is thus in itself an independent democracy, or rather, it has no supremacy exercised over it, but the supremacy of Christ. It acknowledges no authority under Christ to be higher than itself, in reference to its own duties. Prelatic orders and legislative Assemblies are alike repudiated, on the ground that Christ has established no such vicarship over his heritage. Associations and Unions may meet for conference upon Christian work, but they can exercise no governmental functions. Individual churches are the highest executives of Christ on earth. If an offending brother hear not the church, there is no higher court of appeal. An aggregation of churches can have no dominion over the faith of an individual church. If a church do err from the faith, sister churches may labor for its reclamation, but can exercise over it no coercive power. Their only course in cases of persistent error is simply a withdrawal of church fellowship. Yet while Regular Baptist Churches are mutually independent they may consistently seek counsel, one from another, in times of difficulty. Nor does their independency absolve them from the claim of common honesty that each do consider the interests and opinions of sister churches as well as its own, in all matters which may in any way affect the general well-being. Nor does this independency in any way hinder sister churches from uniting, by mutual consent, on a basis of common faith, for the advancement of all Christian enterprise which requires co-operative labor; and in so far as they unite for mutual co-operation, in so far must there be mutual inter-dependency. Thus Regular Baptist Churches, in their independency, possess all the advantages of individual freedom and united strength.

Another essential and distinctive principle which characterizes an organized body of Christians, as a Regular Baptist Church, is *absolute non-interference with divine institutions.*

This holds true in reference to the laws which Christ has instituted for the government of His Kingdom. Regular Baptist Churches maintain that Church legislation is not only unnecessary, but that any attempt in this direction is a daring assumption of the prerogatives of the King of Zion. Christ is sole Legislator. The laws of His Kingdom are already established by Himself. His churches are called upon not to enact laws for self-government, but simply to observe all things whatsoever He has commanded. The authority with which His churches are invested is simply executive. So emphatically does Christ forbid any interference with the laws which He has instituted that He declares the person who presumes to make even the slightest alteration, if he be Christian at all, to be the lowest subject in His realm. Whosoever, therefore, shall break one of these least commandments, and shall teach men so, he shall be called the least in the Kingdom of Heaven. In the light of such declaration, every Christian must acknowledge that Divine institutions may not be changed by man. No one who believes the Bible can acknowledge less. But he who makes this acknowledgment thereby surrenders that for which Regular Baptist Churches contend, and must also accept what his acknowledgment involves. Thus, if Divine institutions may not be changed, there follows, first, that the churches of Christ must observe the Christ-established conditions of membership. When Christ, therefore, declares that none but the regenerate may enter the Kingdom, what man dare violate His commands by introducing the unregenerate ? When Christ institutes baptism as His ordinance, who may change it to sprinkling ? When Christ says that none but believers are fit subjects for Christian baptism, who may add, "and their children ? "

But further, he who admits, as every Christian must, that man has no right to interfere with Divine institutions, must accept another conclusion which this acknowledgment involves, and, in so doing, must abandon every position on which open communion rests. If Christ has established an order in the observance of gospel ordinances, man may no more violate that order than he may violate any other of the institutions of God. That Christ has established order in the gospel system is seen from the fact that regeneration, by his command, precedes baptism, and baptism, by his command, precedes church-fellowship. But, if baptism precedes church-fellowship, it must also precede the Lord's Supper, which is observed only within the fellowship of the church. A Regular Baptist Church, therefore, believes, in common with other bodies of Christians, that, in the order of observance, baptism precedes the Lord's Supper. This is the order in which they were instituted by Christ. This is the order in which they stand enjoined in the great commission. This is the order in which they were observed in the apostolic practice. Here, then, is the real question at issue between Regular Baptist churches and open communionists: "Shall we keep the ordinances as they were delivered?" But, if it be true, as we have already shown, that there must be absolutely no interference with divine institutions, how can we, in God's name, invite to a course which is subversive of divinely established order? Examine the statue book of the King of Zion and if you can find one instance in which He has, either my precept or example, reversed the order which He instituted in the observance of the ordinances, then take that single exception and argue from it against the general law. But if there be not, as there is not in the Word of God, a single recorded example where the Lord's Supper preceded baptism, then those who fight against this order are simply at war with the Almighty. The man who hurls his censures against the observance of this rule must remember that he implicates thereby, not the subject whose duty is obedience, but the great Lawgiver Himself, and thus, with imputations of unchristian narrowness, assails the character of the Most High. The test of the communion question, as of every other article of Christian faith and practice, is not personal feeling, but the Word of God. So far as personal feelings are concerned, Regular Baptist Churches cherish Christian love toward every Christian denomination, but they do not believe that they are called upon to give expression to that love by breaking the laws of Christ, nor do they think him fit for communion who would seek it by such a means. They believe that the truest love to God and man is that which, even amid misrepresentations and censure, preserves inviolate so divine a gift as gospel truth. They therefore accept and assert, as an indispensable principle in the constitution of a truly scriptural church, absolute non-interference with divine institutions.

Thus I have spoken what, to me, appears essential to Regular Baptist Church existence. I take it that no body is a truly Regular Baptist Church where any of these principles is wanting. I take that body to be a Regular Baptist Church where all these principles are found united. I have not spoken these beliefs in the hope of their universal acceptance, nor have I spoken them with any other prompting than that of sincerest conviction. If my statements are incorrect, let them be proved so, and no one will be more grateful than I for their refutation. If they are correct, as I believe they are, then I leave them with you to be maintained.

# THE INSPIRED ESTIMATE OF ORTHODOXY.*

A low human estimate of orthodoxy is the present curse of Christendom. Every department of religious thought and feeling is marked by a carelessness of theological belief. The loose-reined speculation, now so prevalent in reference to fundamental doctrines, would find a much narrower limit, if there were a higher reverence for truth. Doubt may, for a time, take possession of the sincerest mind, but while it remained doubt, it would never be flung broad-cast upon the world by anyone who had any just appreciation of sound doctrine. While there is real earnestness for human salvation in the great evangelistic movement of the present day, there is yet an utter recklessness of correct belief. How many are ready to praise the liberality of him who can say, "If you are only converted I care not what church you join." Yet those who are pleased with this sentiment know full well that the fundamental doctrines held by one denomination are flatly denied by another, and that therefore the beliefs of both cannot be true. The human estimate of uncorrupted doctrine is so low, that utter indifference as to whether men hold truth or error is accounted a perfection of Christian life. How many look with careless eye upon the rending of the seamless robe of truth, into what are called its essential and non-essential parts! How many are ready to in-

---

*Valedictory Address, Woodstock College, 1878.

11

dulge in a sweet self-complacency, because they can find it in themselves to sacrifice their sincerest convictions, upon the altar of a falsely-named Christian charity! Let us turn from such grovelling valuation of correct belief and view the Inspired Estimate of Orthodoxy.

We read this estimate in the care taken to impart correct doctrinal knowledge. For thousands of years the world was undergoing a course of preparation for the reception of the truth. Language was brought to its highest degree of perfection, that it might be a vehicle fit for such a communication. Then the great Instructor appears upon the scene, commissioned to teach men definite doctrines. He bears with him the credentials which attest his divine authority. While he repeats and enforces the lessons he would impart, he, yet, abides so closely by the letter of the Father's commandment, that in closing his earthly ministry he can say : I have given unto them the very words which thou hast given me. Though his presence is dearer than life to his people, he tells them that there is an end to be gained by his departure, which makes it better for them that he should go away. The end in view is, that, by another course of teaching, they may be led into all the truth. He proves his estimate of his doctrine, in that he dies a martyr to the truths he proclaimed. As he is about to seal his testimony with his blood, he thus emphatically declares the great purpose of his mission : "To this end was I born, and for this cause came I into the world, that I should bear witness to the truth." Another Person of the

divine trinity is now commissioned to carry on the
work begun. He is to lead his followers, not so much
into new fields of thought, as to bring to their remembrance, and unfold to them, the truths already delivered. To guard against any possibility of change
or loss, he gives a written record for all time. In this
work he makes choice of the human mind as a me-
dium, so that truth imparted through the ordinary
channels of communication may be understood by all.
He makes use of various minds, so that, by every
style of thought, men may apprehend more closely his
meaning. He so guides each chosen writer, by his
own immediate influence, as to secure an unerring
testimony to his people, and then pledges his presence
to them forever, to guide them into all the truth revealed. This wondrous course of instruction, undertaken in order that men might know the truth, reveals
the inspired estimate of a correct knowledge of divine
things.

The high value attached, by the divine mind, to
orthodoxy is seen in the means employed to perpetu-
ate its existence. The church is made the pillar and
ground of truth in the world. Her glorious work is
to preserve and extend the knowledge of the truth.
For this purpose the gifts of the Spirit are lavished
upon her. There are given unto her apostles, prophets,
evangelists, pastors and teachers, that, thus edified,
she may be strong "in the unity of the faith," un-
moved by the shifting winds of false doctrine. Those
who have embraced the truth are commanded to hold
it fast, to keep it pure, to receive from neither man

nor angel any contrary teaching. They are bidden to part with all things else, if need be, for its sake, but on no condition to part with the truth : to die for it rather than renounce it.   He who thus commits the sacred trust to his people's keeping declares his excellence, in that he has given to it immutability.   No other system shall supersede the form of doctrine delivered.   No change shall be wrought in it.   The most solemn threatenings are recorded against any who would dare to take from, or add to, its divine perfection.   That the world may know the exceeding preciousness of the doctrines which Christ has taught, he contrasts them with all created things, and shows their pre-eminent value, in that he accords to them alone perpetual existence.   " Heaven and earth shall pass away, but my words shall not pass away."

The inspired estimate of orthodoxy is seen in the position assigned to it, in the scheme of redemption. All the vital interests of the Christian religion are secured to man on no other condition.   Salvation is dependent upon, and effected through, belief of the truth.   One of the degenerate tendencies of the age, arising, in part, out of a misapprehension of the source of power in the present evangelical movement, is to accept the fervid utterances of false doctrines as a means through which conversion may be wrought, as if human earnestness could accomplish the work of the living word.   Let the Church of God cease to dishonor the truth.   Sincerity is not orthodoxy.   If sincere belief were an equivalent for correct doctrine, then might the very devotees of heathenism ascend in

he chariots of salvation even to the throne of God.
Earnestness has no efficacy in itself.   Gospel doctrine
is the only means of gospel blessing.   Error may be a
factor in man's creed, but it can be no factor in his
salvation.   The truth, the truth only, the truth rightly
apprehended, is that by which a soul is saved.

In the work of sanctification the same instrumen-
tality is used.   It is by the clear light of truth that
the great artist photographs the divine image upon
the soul.   It is by the power of Christian doctrine,
operating upon the heart, that we have the result of
Christian character and life.   Men may say, "It makes
little difference what man believes providing he lives
right."   Such empty philosophy amounts to no more
than this, that, there is no necessity for a cause, so
long as we have an effect.   The only possibility of
right life is through belief of the truth.   That man
may be "perplexed in faith, but pure in deeds" is a
statement which receives little sanction from divine
authority.   The fruit of perfect deeds is not a growth
from doubtful principles.   "Either make the tree
good and his fruit good, or else make the tree corrupt
and his fruit corrupt."   The faith which purifies the
heart is not that which rests on false assumptions,
not even that which dwells in "honest doubt," but that
which draws its life from the uncorrupted spring.
The sanctification of the Spirit is through belief of
the truth.

Apart from sound doctrine, there can be no God-
accepted service in life.   This is not saying that a
perfect knowledge of all revealed truth is necessary

to any single act of Christian worship, but that the sphere of acceptable service is limited to that of apprehended truth. If the object of our worship be not the God of the Bible, but merely our mistaken notions of deity, then we bow down to a god of our creation. The object is false, and the homage rendered, however sincere and correct in itself, is nothing but idolatry. If, having a true knowledge of God, we adopt other forms of worship than those which he has enjoined, then the service is false, and however devoutly offered can be nothing but an abomination. The human estimate of orthodoxy may be so low, that men may think lightly of having violated the perfection of the divine arrangement; but God says, "In vain do they worship me, teaching for doctrines the commandments of men."

Orthodoxy is given as the only bond of Christian union. The attempt to effect harmony in the Christian world on any other basis, either by a compromise with error, or by a suppression of principle, is an unhallowed experiment, altogether foreign to the truth-loving spirit of the Gospel. Truth and error can never be made one. Such unholy wedlock of what God hath not joined together is not Christian union. It is false in name, and false in principle. The fellowship of saints is a fellowship of heart, in truth, not a sinful reticence of belief. It is not by concealing differences, but by coming to the truth, that the church is to gain her real concord. Departure from the truth is the cause of all the schisms in Christendom. A return to the uncorrupted faith can be the only cure. He, who steadfastly opposes error, and faithfully declares all the truth, may be branded as narrow and sectarian, but he is really the true champion of Christian union. The divided Church of God cannot be one till it finds completeness "in the unity of faith."    In the fact that salvation, sanctification, all acceptable service, and all real Christian union, are conditioned, for all time, and for all people, upon belief of the truth, we read once more the high importance attached to orthodoxy, by Him whose estimate is infallible.

The corroborative testimony to this written esti- mate is given, by the Spirit, in the whole history of the church.    Truth believed and proclaimed is that alone by which the divine conquests are effected. None other than the living blade is acknowledged by the hand of Him whose might alone can give success.    The sword of the Spirit is the word of God.  How he proves the power of this weapon through all time !   A few fishermen are called from their nets, and, by the sim- ple declaration of the truth, they shake the world as conqueror never shook it before.   While that truth is held uncorrupted the church advances, nor can the combined opposition of all her foes retard her pro- gress.    But when once the standards of orthodoxy are fallen, she sinks, nevertheless, into the darkness of the middle ages.   Once more the Reformers lay firm hold upon the great doctrines of the Gospel.   The same accounts which first shook the world are heard again.    They are the very trumpet-blast of heaven summoning divine might to the conflict.   The Spirit acknowledges the truth and the world trembles before his power.   Through all subsequent time the same invariable testimony is given. Every awakening of Christian life and thought that marks the centuries, every conquest that the church has effected in the world, has been accomplished through the truth. Lest such results should be attributed to mere human power, lofty genius is permitted to exhaust itself in fruitless effort, while attempting reformation by "enticing words of man's wisdom." Then the divine Spirit compels acknowledgment of the superiority of gospel doctrine, in that he sends it forth dependent on no excellency of speech, to revolutionize the world.

While the worth of orthodoxy is thus clearly attested, what more execrable daring, than that the professed ambassador from God to men should tone down the message fraught with life and death, lest it might grate too harshly upon the ears and hearts of those to whom it is delivered ? What more sinful presumption than to venture change in any department of Jehovah's plan ? Ye who are musicians, what think ye of the mere juvenile performer who would throw in his own variations, while attempting to render the sublimest strains of Handel or Mozart ? Ye who are painters, what think ye of the raw beginner who would daub the finished works of Raphael into his own ideas of perfection ? Ye who are Christians, what think ye of the finite creature who would dare to work his own ideas of improvement upon the crowning effort of infinite skill ? It is not a small thing, that men should apply the distorting rack of a biased mind to the faultless form of truth, and mar its God-given beauty. It is not a thing of little moment, that men should fail to embrace any part of truth, or, by specious argument, lead others from it. When the divine Instructor propounded the laws of the kingdom he was about to establish, he said, that he who would break one of the least of his commands, and teach men to do so, should be least in His kingdom; but that he who obeyed and taught His commands, should be accounted great. While this simple condition of divine approval and preferment is thus plainly declared, by Him who is king in Zion, if we prize the honor which cometh from above, let us strive to win it, by holding fast, and holding forth, the truth as it is in Jesus. Let us scorn the attempt to attract human attention by mere novelty of thought. Let it be ours to proclaim "the truth, the whole truth and nothing but the truth." Let it be our high ambition, as it is our highest honor, to hold taintless and intact the doctrines committed to our trust, to contend earnestly for the faith delivered once for all.

---

## A HOME MISSION ADDRESS.*

"Every place whereon the soles of your feet shall tread shall be yours,"—this was God's word to the ancient people. The Holy Land of promise lay before them, and "every place whereon the soles of your feet shall tread,"—this was the extent of their possibility. "Every place whereon the soles of your feet shall

*Delivered at the Convention, in 1882.

tread,"—this was the simple condition of conquest
and possession. This also was the unqualified assurance of success : every place thus occupied shall be
yours. Such is our own position. As a denomination
we stand with our fair land of promise before us. We
have received of God the right of possession, the title
deeds of truth. And how shall we enter upon the
inheritance ? Again the divine conditions are presented. Make it yours by possession. "Every place
whereon the soles of your feet shall tread shall be
yours." However correct may be our faith, however
important may be our principles, they shall never extend in our land apart from our effort. Let us be confident as we may in the ultimate triumph of truth,
yet that triumph will never be achieved apart from
the agency divinely appointed. If our faith is to
spread in our country it must do so through our Home
Mission enterprise. Principles if they are to prevail
must be propagated by those who hold them. Observation and experience reveal no other method of progress. There are two factors recognizable in every
advance of doctrine, whether that doctrine be true or
false. One fact is the creed itself, the other is the
human agency by which it is promulgated. Principles
are not epidemic, but are spread through the conta-
gious influence of mind on mind. Let a doctrine be
absolute truth and let it cease to be proclaimed and it
becomes a forgotten thing. Yet at the same time the
most egregious system of error in the world to-day
flourishes, propagates itself through the zeal of those
who espouse it. Read the history of any movement

whether in secular or religious thought, and there
stand before you the living advocates as truly as the
principles for which they contended.  The principles
of free trade were as true through the centuries that
England starved herself by wretched corn-laws, as
they were in the middle of the present century, when
she repealed them and made the world's granaries
contributory to her people's good.  The principles she
then accepted were as true before their adoption as
they were then and are now, but they would have
slumbered forever had not men arisen and advocated
them, and thus agitated and enlightened the public
mind, and enabled England to proudly lead the van
of nations in the grand march of economic science.
The birthright of human freedom was man's inalien-
able possession from the beginning, but that birthright
was not acknowledged or accorded, even in the hands
of boasted civilization, till Wilberforce advocated
emancipation for England, and in America Lincoln
spoke freedom to the slave.  Justification by faith
was a truth as old as the gospel, but it needed the
energies of a Luther and of his fellow-reformers to
drag it from the darkness of papal error, and to thrust
it forth upon a world that lay in spiritual darkness.
The history of truth reveals no other method whereby
we may propagate the faith of our church, the faith
of the gospel in our land.  If we would propagate it,
we must proclaim it.  In the nature of things there
can be progress for us only as we disseminate the
truth.  In the physical world there can be no growth
of fruit if the seed be not planted in the soil.  Grain

the most living and productive may be stored in barns
of plenty, but it cannot multiply till it is taken forth
and sown upon the fields.    In the same way our
churches may be possessed of the precious seed, even
the incorruptible seed of the word which liveth and
abideth forever, but they may not expect to multiply
and fill the land unless they cast forth that seed upon
the fields which lie open to their toil and care.    In
the realm of secular education the growth in knowledge is by teaching.    Truth must be presented before
it can be received.    It is different in spiritual things?
Does not faith come by hearing, and hearing by the
word of God? Our faith must be known before it
can be accepted.    How can they believe that which
they have not heard, and how can they hear without
a preacher, and how can they preach except they be
sent?    God never designed that His truth should advance otherwise than through the advocacy of them
that hold it; it has pleased Him through the foolishness of preaching to save them that believe.    Ye are
the light of the world.    God's angel may go to the
house of Cornelius to tell him that his prayers and his
alms are come up for a memorial, but it is not his to
instruct him in the words of truth and life.    This is
reserved for human agency.    "Send men to Joppa to
inquire for one Simon whose surname is Peter; he
shall tell thee what thou oughtest to do."    There is
but one agency appointed, as truly as there is but one
gospel to proclaim.    If our Home Mission fields are
ever to receive our principles, they must receive them
at our hands.    Nor is the fact that other denomina-

tions occupy these fields a reason why we should not
enter. We really owe the proclamation of our faith
to our God and to our country. If it is God's truth
we surely need not be ashamed to obtrude it upon
the attention of other denominations. God's word
needs no apology for its entrance into any community,
and if it ever is to have prevalence, it must be introduced by those who hold it. It would ·be a libel and a
sin against the truth-loving spirit of scientific inquiry
to keep back the light of advancing knowledge lest it
might overthrow some theories already accepted. The
cry of every truth-loving spirit would be, " Let in the
light, let in the light." However much it might conflict with cherished opinion, the truths of revelation
are infinitely more important and needful to man
than the truths of science. He would be a traitor to
that truth, to the highest interests of his country,
whose false courtesy would advise non-entrance upon
such fields of missionary enterprise. If then our principles are to advance in Home fields, we must plant
new causes, and of necessity plant them in weakness,
and care for them till they grow to strength. The
trees that are planted in the rainless deserts must not
only be borne thither for plantation, but must be
watered copiously and continuously by those who
have planted them, till their roots take deep hold
upon the soil and their leafy branches spread out
towards heaven. But let this work be done, and there
comes a time when it will repay labor ; there comes a
time when these trees will reclaim the desert by at-
tracting the rains of heaven and thus turning the

barren solitudes into fields of fruitfulness. So in
Christian enterprise, we must bear the truth to the
fields that are needy and sustain the causes planted
in weakness, till they rise to strength and reclaim the
deserts by bringing the spiritual wastes under the
power of gospel husbandry, and calling down there
the times of refreshing that come from the presence
of the Lord. The denomination that does not propagate its principles must die. In this day of high
pressure in business enterprise, no one need hope for
success in such a calling who resigns himself to ease
and indolence. The reins of trade are grasped and
held by those who are enthusiastic in their departments, who are ready to endure the mental strain, to
watch for opportunities and meet them with means
commensurate to their undertakings. So also it is in
the fields of Christian endeavor, where the keenness
and rivalry of denominational competitions prevail.
The body that will not rise to lay hold of the opportunities of progress must sink to relative insignifi-
cance. Though for a time there may not be numerical
decrease in a body that fails to lay hold of fresh
ground, yet if it fail to make progress, while other
denominations are pressing onward with rapid marches
and occupying extended fields of Christian enterprise,
it must become relatively weaker and must accept a
position of comparative obscurity. Still further, let
a denomination fail to make progress while others are
advancing with rapid strides, and even its own adher-
ents will lose faith in it. That which remains at a
standstill in a day of activity ceases to have inspira-

tion and is soon relegated to the past. Let a school
of training that holds a foremost position neglect its
work and make a poor record, while competing colleges are winning high distinction, and it thereby
blasts its highest possibilities. It has lost that pres-
tige which was an essential element in its prosperity
—an element moreover which is much more easily
lost than won. The principle is true in its application
in every department of life, "There is nothing suc-
ceeds like success"; and there is nothing fails like
failure. It may be objected that it is a worthless
gain to enlightened Christian principle which is drawn
merely by attraction. The objection would be valid
if there were nothing further contemplated for those
who are thus brought within the reach of influence.
But while a denomination draws by its popularity, it
thus gains the best opportunity to mould by its teachings, and so attach by the power of principle, those
who were at first drawn only by the magnetism of
success. Thus the fields of Home Mission toil which
give to our churches the possibility of extended influence in the land, are those that, when occupied, must
by that influence, re-act powerfully for the well-being
of those who have planted them. There is that scattereth and yet increaseth, and there is that withholdeth
more than is meet and it tendeth to poverty. In the
very nature of things the body that does not cultivate
the missionary spirit cannot expect to live, for if the
Spirit does anything it imparts the spirit of missions.
The denomination that does not propagate its principles abroad must die at home. He that saveth his

life shall lose it, and he that loseth his life in gospel
enterprise the same shall find it.    The liberal soul
deviseth liberal things, and by liberal things shall he
stand.    The propagation of principles apart from the
liberal consecration of means is an impossibility.    No
company on earth could expect to establish and extend new branches of its industry and equip them for
efficient service without expending much capital upon
the enterprise.    England's late campaign in the East
for the restoration of law and order could never have
been a possibility apart from her readiness to meet all
necessary demands on men and toil and treasure.    Even
if it be but a short political contest in our country,
that party cannot expect to find its principles domi-
nant, which makes no sacrifice for their lawful advocacy.    The Church of God, divinely inaugurated for
the spread of the gospel, can in this respect be no
exception.    Her principles cannot prevail apart from
the contribution of the gold and silver that are needful for dissemination.    "Bring ye all the tithes into
the storehouse that there may be meat in my house,
and prove me now herewith, saith the Lord of Hosts,
if I will not open you the windows of heaven and
pour you out a blessing that there shall not be room
enough to receive it."    While God himself thus calls
us to the acceptance and proof of his conditions and
blessing, while the opening fields of our country are
crying to us for laborers, while principles purchased
by the death of Christ and held through the centuries
by the blood of saints are ours for propagation, we
prize not as we ought the sacred trust.    We prove

ourselves unworthy of so divine an honor, if now, in the day of our highest possibilities, we strive not to plant the faith of our churches in the hearts and homes of our country.

---

## MAN'S QUESTIONINGS ABOUT GOD'S PROMISES.*

Whatsoever ye shall ask in my name, that will I do.  If ye shall ask anything in my name, I will do it.  Jno. xiv : 13-14.  How can these things be ?  Jno. iii : 9.

I do not place these texts together because of any special connection of thought existing between them, but simply to suggest some of man's questionings in reference to God's promises.  The pledge here given is startling in its freeness and its vastness, and man unaccustomed to such liberality, overborne by its magnitude may be led almost to doubt its genuineness.  If this promise be true, then nothing is too great to ask.  No petition can be too all-embracing, for no creature can stretch the arms of faith beyond the bounds of this declaration.  "Whatsoever," without any limitation, "whatsoever ye shall ask in My name, that will I do."  Nor, on the other hand, can there be any want or difficulty too small to bring to God in prayer.  The child can bow down before the throne of grace lisping his little troubles with the assurance that they are not too small to engage the attention of Him who made and who rules the worlds

---

*A Sermon preached before the Midland Counties Association, in 1882.

12

There is nothing beneath his notice, " If ye shall ask anything in My name, I will do it." Or man may come in the maturity of his power, when his best efforts have been baffled, knowing assuredly that there is not a perplexity too dark or a need too great to bring in faith and hope before the Father of spirits. In the blackest night of human sorrow, when life like a troubled sea beats its rock-bound coast in wild unrest, then in the midst of my distresses I will come to thee, O Thou whose arm is strong to save. When all creature aid is unavailing, then I will rise and take hold on the Almighty. From the ends of the earth I will cry unto thee, " When my heart is overwhelmed within me, lead me unto the rock that is higher than I." Nor shall I seek thine offered aid in vain, for thou hast said, " Whatsoever ye shall ask in My name that will I do. If ye shall ask anything in My name I will do it." Nor do these promises refer to spiritual blessings only. They cover all human need. There is not a real want in human experience, but comes justly within the embrace of their limitless assurance. They that trust in the Lord shall not want any good thing. My God shall supply all your need according to his riches in glory, by Christ Jesus. There is absolutely no good thing in God's universe, that is placed beyond the reach of believing prayer. Here are the divine promises : " Whatsoever ye shall ask in My name, that I will do. If ye shall ask anything in My name, I will do it." Here too is the human questioning in reference to them : " How can these things be ?" Let us strive to-day to meet some of man's questionings in reference to God's promises and the efficacy of prayer. The first and humbler phase of unbelief is that of

I. *Doubting the availability of the divine promises, through a sense of personal unworthiness.*

In this form of doubt, the validity of the promises remains unquestioned. The enquirer heartily acknowledges that they are worthy of all acceptation, but distrusts his own interest in them. The promises are worthy, all-worthy, but self-unworthiness forbids appropriation. The difficulty here presented is not imaginary. The Christian hears the voice of Christ saying, "Whatsoever ye shall ask in My name, that will I do," but while he asks, he is conscious that his expectations are not equal to the promise given. It is not easy to lift undeserving hands and lay hold, with confidence, on so rich an inheritance. This form of doubt is almost inevitable in Christian experience. Are the exceeding great and precious promises of God unlimitedly mine? Am I called to the throne of grace and irrespective of any personal merit bidden to ask whatsoever I will? How can these things be?

(*a*) These things can be, because the economy under which the promises are given is one of grace. If it were one of works, then its promises would be, "Whatsoever ye have earned that shall ye receive." But since it is one of grace its blessings are no longer conditioned upon or measured by human merit, but are just as free and as vast as is the sovereign favour of God. The doubt that rests on self-judgment is misplaced. Man cannot argue his possibilities from the premises of personal merit, for they are not the condition of his acceptance. Merit he has none, but the King, who has a right to do what he will with his own may be graciously pleased in the exercise of his sovereignty, to bestow blessings where they are unmerited. Thus the promises which are utterly inconsistent with a system of works are perfectly consistent with a system of sovereign grace The extent of man's possibility is the extent of divine favour and the extent of this favour is read in the proclaimed will of the King, " Whatsoever ye shall ask in My name, that will I do."

(b) These things can be, because the Christian asks in the name of Him who has purchased the promised blessings. The infinite merits of Jesus Christ are the accepted purchase-price of all the possible good that God can bestow upon his people. He who goes by the authority of Christ to the mercy-seat and there asks in Jesus' name for purchased and promised blessing, may do so in all the confidence that the worth of Christ can inspire. When a Rothschild signs a cheque it makes no difference whether he be a pauper or a king who presents it at the banking-house for acknowledgment. The draft is honored, not because of any real or supposed worth in him who presents the paper, but solely for the value of the name it bears. So the Christian who comes to the throne of grace, finds his petitions honored, not because of his personal excellency, but solely in virtue of the name he pleads. Verily, verily, I say unto you, whatsoever ye shall ask the Father in My name, He will give it you.

(c) These things can be, for the Almighty can know
no limitation in the fulfilment of his promises.   He is
able to do exceeding abundantly above all that we
are able to ask or think.   Moreover, his willingness is
not less than his ability.   God delights in giving.   All
his works, in all places of his dominion, receive from
him all that they are and all that they enjoy.   But
there are no creatures in his universe that he more
delights to bless than his people.   His love to his
children will not suffer them to want any good thing.
Here is the resistless logic of his own word : If ye
being evil know how to give good gifts to your children, how much more will your Father which is in
heaven give good things to them that ask him ?   He
that spared not his own Son, but delivered him up for
us all, how shall he not with him also freely give us
all things ?   Surely then this first phase of doubt is
answered.   The promises of God are available, to their
utmost extent, for all his people. Whatsoever ye shall
ask in my name, that will I do.

The second and darker form of unbelief, in reference to the divine promises and Christian prayer, is

II. *Doubting the possibility of their fulfilment
through the limitations of human knowledge.*

The question no longer is, whether these exceeding
great and precious promises are available for me, but,
can God make good his word ?   The doubt here is in
reference to the validity of the divine promises, because man can see no way whereby God can fulfil
them.   Christ says, "Whatsoever ye shall ask in My

name, that will I do. If ye shall ask anything in My
name, I will do it," and man responds, "How can
these things be ?" How can such unqualified promises
be made good ?   How can my asking have any influence upon the divine mind ?   If God engages to hear
all prayer, how can he govern the universe with fixed
laws ?—I cannot reconcile such a promise with his
pre-arranged schemes of providence, and therefore I
doubt its possibility.   Show me some way whereby
the fulfilment of such a promise is possible, and I will
not withhold trust, but on no other condition will I
yield belief.   Here is the darker form of doubt.   Because I cannot understand the ways of the Almighty,
I will therefore doubt his declarations.   Because I can
see no way whereby he can fulfil his promises, I will
therefore doubt the all-prevalence he has attached to
prayer, " Except I see I will not believe."

(a) The unwarrantable folly of such pretentious
doubt is not far to seek.   Man need not think that,
where his little knowledge strikes its boundary, he
has found a limit beyond which the Almighty cannot
cross.   Even if man should find himself shut up to
inevitable contradictions, in his attempts to conceive
how Jehovah can fulfil his promises, he surely cannot
think that, therefore, there is no way possible to God.
Until the finite can comprehend the infinite, man need
not expect to rest his faith in God's ability to do what
he promises, on man's finite and imperfect knowledge
of what is possible.   My ways are not your ways,
neither are your thoughts my thoughts, saith the
Lord, for as the heavens are higher than the earth, so

are my ways higher than your ways and my thoughts than your thoughts.  O the depth of the riches both of the wisdom and knowledge of God ! how unsearchable are his judgments and his ways past finding out. The limitations of man's knowledge are no boundaries of divine possibility.  They are, therefore, not the boundaries of Christian faith, and they afford no reason for questioning the validity of the divine promises.

*(b)* Again, man finds, day by day, that seeming impossibilities are rendered possible by man.  That a surgeon could amputate a limb from the human body and the patient feel no pain during the operation, would have been laughed at as an impossibility, until it became a fact through scientific achievement.  That man should be able to transmit messages to the uttermost parts of the earth in the space of a few minutes, would have been deemed a thing incredible, until the electric telegraph proved the possibility beyond all contradiction.    While advancing knowledge shows thus, in ten thousand cases, that long-supposed impossibilities are possible and easy to him that understandeth, need man wonder that he whose knowledge is perfect should have some way of accomplishing His purposes, even though that way may not be open to human sight ?

*(c)* Nor is this claiming anything which is not again proved by the facts of inspired history.  Abraham might have doubted the divine promise which was given to him when he was about an hundred years old, for the human conditions under which it was spoken were such as would argue impossibility.  But

the father of the faithful never dreamed of measuring
God's power by man's knowledge of what was possible.
Looking unto the promise of God he wavered not
through unbelief, but waxed strong through faith
giving glory to God, being fully persuaded that what
God had promised he was able also to perform.   Man
could not have told how God could justify a sinner
whom his law condemned, while that sinner could
provide no righteousness and while that law could not
relax its claims.   The challenge might have been
thrown out, "How can man be just with God?"
"How can this thing be?"   Yet God has made plain
to the simplest understanding the way whereby he
can be just and yet the justifier of the ungodly. Christ
said to his disciples, "It is easier for a camel to go
through the eye of a needle than for a rich man to
enter into the kingdom of God."   The disciples, astonished beyond measure, exclaim, "Who then can be
saved?"   The answer is simply this, "With men it is
impossible but not with God, for with God all things
are possible."   So Christ says, "Whatsoever ye shall
ask in My name, that will I do.   If ye shall ask anything in My name, I will do it."   Does man question
"How can these things be?"   Does he doubt these
promises because the possibility of their fulfilment
transcends the limitations of human knowledge?   Be
it so: this is no objection to their validity, for the
things that are impossible with men are possible with
God.

The third and darkest stage of doubt in reference
to God's promises and the efficacy of prayer, is

III. *Declaring the impossibility of their fulfilment
on the ground that they are contradicted by human
knowledge.*

Here, in this darkest form of doubt, unbelief grows
positive and not simply questions, but denies, the validity of the divine promises and the efficacy of prayer.
The objection no longer rests on the limitations of
human knowledge, but upon its supposed sufficiency.
Man imagines that he has involved the Almighty in
contradictions.   He now questions thus :   Are these
promises verified in experience ?   As a matter of fact
does God grant unto his people whatsoever they ask ?
Have not God's people often, in tearful anxiety, prayed
for the recovery of a loved one from death and yet no
recovery came ?   Have not his people often in perplexity in the business of life, asked him to help
them through a financial crisis and yet they have
become insolvent even in the midst of their askings,
and that too in the face of the reiterated declaration,
"Whatsoever ye shall ask in My name, that will I
do.   If ye shall ask anything in My name, I will do
it."   Does this plain promise meet its fulfilment in
experience ?   Still further, how can God fulfil this
promise, while he governs the world by unchangeable
laws ?   Can he promise to grant whatsoever his people may ask, when that asking may not be in accordance with his unchangeable will ?   If this be the
form of doubt presented, then let us seek its answer.

(*a*) Let us recognize first that these promises are
made only to true prayer.   Christ does not pledge

himself to answer every petition that man may offer,
but every petition that is offered in his name. His
merit is the only condition on which prayer may be
answered. God grants his favors to man for Jesus'
sake. For how many soever be the promises of God
in him is the Yea; wherefore also through him is the
Amen. Before man presumes to question the faithfulness of God's promises to prayer, let him first en-
quire, what prayer is that which God has promised to
answer? Certainly not every desire that man may
breathe before the throne of grace. Certainly not all
prayer that is characterized by sincerity and fervor.
Christ has not promised this. But, Whatsoever ye
shall ask *in My name*—mark the condition—*in My
name,*—Whatsoever ye shall ask in My name, that
will I do. If ye shall ask anything in My name, I
will do it. The promise is limited to that which is
offered up by faith, in Jesus' name. He never came
in Jesus' name who came not in faith, and he never
came in faith who came not in Jesus' name, and without faith it is impossible to please God. Man cannot
go to him and ask for a blessing to see if there be
truth in his promise. He must believe. The man
who goes in faith will return saying, "It was just as
I expected," and the man who goes without faith will
return saying, "It was just as I expected," for let not
that man think that he shall receive anything from
the Lord. But whatsoever ye shall ask in faith, believing, that ye shall receive. The first step in the
answer to the objection presented, then, is this. These
promises are given not to every petition, but only to

true prayer, that is, to prayer offered through, in, Jesus' name.

*(b)* The second step in the argument is this. There can be no true prayer without the aid of the Holy Spirit. Man cannot draw nigh unto God apart from the Spirit's leading. Even the taking of the name of God acceptably upon our lips is his gift. He is the Spirit of adoption whereby we cry, Abba, Father. "Our Father who art in heaven," is a cry which no human heart can raise, except as the Spirit of adoption voices it with us. But because ye are sons, God hath sent forth the Spirit of the Son into our hearts, crying, Abba, Father. Thus we cannot call upon God in prayer apart from the aid of the Holy Spirit. Again, the reasons which give acceptance to any petitions at the throne of grace, are such as prove that there can be no true prayer without the Holy Spirit's aid. The infinite merits of the incarnate Saviour form the basis of all true prayer. No man can expect blessing if he ask it not in the name of Jesus Christ as his Lord. And no man can so ask apart from the assistance of the Holy Spirit, for no man calleth Jesus Lord, but by the Holy Ghost. Still further, our weakness and ignorance are such that we know not what petitions to present before the throne of grace. We know not how or what to pray for as we ought. But the Spirit helps our infirmities, he maketh intercession for us and within us with groanings that cannot be uttered, and thus enables us to pray. The desire for prayer, the desire for holiness and every good and perfect gift received through prayer, is the Holy Spirit's creation.

He works in us both to will and to do, to ask and to receive, according to his good pleasure. Thus we are entirely indebted to the Holy Spirit, for the ability to call God our Father, to call Jesus Christ our Lord, for the inclination to pray and for the intercession by which he enables us to offer acceptable prayer. It is evident therefore that there can be no true prayer without his aid.

(c) But, a third step in the argument. He who thus intercedes within us makes intercession for the saints according to the will of God, even as he himself is God. This intercession of God the Spirit, in man, breathed before the throne of grace, from human hearts, constitutes the sum of all true prayer, even as no true prayer is offered without his aid. But all prayer, thus offered, is in accordance with the will of God, is in line with his unchanging purpose, and will meet its answer as surely as the divine purpose meets its fulfilment. This then is the conclusion. The promises of God are only given to true prayer. All true prayer is by the Holy Spirit's aid. All true prayer is therefore in accordance with God's will. Whatsoever is thus asked, that, says Christ, will I do. This then is the confidence that we have in him, that if we ask anything, according to his will, he heareth us. If ye shall ask anything in My name, I will do it.

I do not say that we are able to distinguish between the prayer that we offer by the Spirit's aid and that which we offer without his aid. We may think that to be true prayer, which is not true prayer. We may think that to be his mind, which is not his mind. Man

knows not, but God knoweth.   He that searcheth the
hearts knoweth what is the mind of the Spirit, because he maketh intercession for the saints according to the will of God.   Nor is such prayer less an
act of man than any other exercise of power.   Every
holy thought, every good desire, that springs in all
freeness and spontaneity from the Christian heart, is
neither more free nor more human than prayer.   All
these things worketh the self-same Spirit, and therefore all these things man is able freely to perform,
since God works in him both to will and to do according to his good pleasure.

IV. *The question then arises, What profit is there
in prayer since it effects no change in the divine
purposes, but asks simply that which God's hand and
God's counsel determined before to be done ?*

I dwell not here on the unspeakable benefits which
are realized through the re-action of prayer upon the
human spirit, but refer only to the power which it
may exert for the obtaining of the direct object
sought.

(*a*) In the first place, he entertains false views of
prayer who looks upon it as a means of effecting
change in the immutable purposes of God.  The design
of prayer is not to inform him of anything which
was before to him unknown.  He, surely, needs not
to borrow information from man wherewith to re-
arrange the all-perfect system of his providence.
Known unto God are all his works from the beginning.   But he who knows all things and has ordered

all things for the highest good, cannot change the
perfection of his purposes, because of the asking of
human short-sightedness and folly.  Prayer may not
then be looked upon as a means by which the mind
of God may be changed.

(b) But he also entertains false views of prayer
who thinks that since it effects no change in God, it
therefore exerts no influence upon him.  The fact
that the premises of God are all divinely connected
with human askings, and that all his highest gifts are
bestowed only in answer to prayer, clearly proves
that prayer does exert some influence upon God.  If
it exerted no influence upon him, it could in no sense
be said to prevail with him.  Influence it exerts, but
that influence is not the influence of change.  It is
the touch of faith which calls forth the blessing God
designs to give.  God is moved by prayer, moved, not
out of the course in which he designs to tread, but
moved in it, to grant unto his people that which he
had purposed for them, in Christ Jesus, before the
world began.  It is poor philosophy to argue that
there is no value in prayer, since all things are certain
to come to pass according to God's unchanging purpose.  All things will not only come to pass as he
designs, but the way in which they will come to pass
will also be as he designs.  He chooses the means by
which a thing shall be, as truly as he chooses that it
shall be.  He leaves nothing to haphazard.  He has
chosen prayer as the means by which he will bestow
blessing.  I the Lord have spoken it, I will do it.  Yet
will I be enquired of by the house of Isreal to do it

for them. He chooses to bless the earth with showers and he will do so, but he has chosen also that he will do it through the earth's own agency. Its power of attraction is that which shall draw the rain-drops to itself. The earth may not say, "I need not exert my force for the rain will descend anyway, since God has willed it." Nay, God has not only willed that the rain shall descend, but also that it shall descend through the exercise of earth's attraction. So God has purposed to out-pour his blessings upon his people, but has designed to do so through the agency of prayer. Ask and it shall be given you. Whatever ye shall ask in My name, that will I do. If ye shall ask anything in My name, I will do it. Thus the verdict of truest reason is one with the voice of Scripture. The conclusion is not that prayer is worthless since no amount of it will change the divine purpose, but, since any amount of prayer carries with it the fulfilment of the divine purpose, therefore it is priceless, for the effectual fervent prayer of a righteous man availeth much.

Here then the unfailing promises of God invite his people to the throne of grace. The darkest questionings of human doubt cannot obscure the light that breaks upon the mercy-seat. The simplest Christian faith is the profoundest of all philosophy. Prayer is the loftiest exercise of human reason. In it man puts forth an energy that is itself divine. By it he prevails with God. "More things are wrought by prayer than this world dreams of."

The world that walks in darkness may question

experiences it has never known, may doubt the validity of the divine promises and the efficacy of believing prayer. But thou, Christian, enter not into the shadow-land of its spectral objections. Enter into thy closet and when thou hast shut to thy door, pray to thy Father which is in secret and he shall recompense thee. In everything by prayer and supplication with thanksgiving, let your requests be made known unto God, for, " Whatsoever ye shall ask in My name, that will I do. If ye shall ask anything in My name, I will do it."

---

## THE HOLY SPIRIT'S AGENCY IN REVIVAL WORK.[*]

If we may distinguish between the work of revivals and ordinary gospel labor, the distinction is not one of different agency or of different operations, but of different degrees in the same methods and by the same agencies. The human and the divine elements in Christian labor are not otherwise associated in revival work than they are in ordinary ministrations. There may be different departments of work and vastly different degrees of success in labor, but in these human and divine elements are not differently related. There are diversities of workings, but all these worketh the one and the same Spirit, dividing to each one severally even as he will. The relation

[*] Published in the *Canadian Baptist*, 1883.

existing between the divine and human workers is
not different in the midst of revival from what it is
in ordinary efforts for human salvation. There certainly is greater intensity of effort at such times on
the part of the human worker, and just as truly is
there greater power of the Spirit crowning Christian
labor, but in each case the difference is one of degree
and not of kind. The agency of the Holy Spirit in
revival work is not the exercise of unusual forces, but
the unusual or higher energies of those continuously
employed. Yet while making no distinction in the
relations of the persons and no distinction in the
modes of operation, but claiming simply for revival
work the higher use of the same powers in the same
relations as are found in ordinary effort, it may be
well to view the Spirit's agency in human salvation
as exhibited in the work of revivals.

*In the first place, the Holy Spirit gives the word of
God, without which revival work is an impossibility.*

No human worker can accomplish anything for the
salvation of men apart from the word of truth, the
gospel of salvation. Man may read God's eternal
power and divinity in the works of creation. He
may preach to men the God of creation, but no revival can possibly be effected through such working.
God in redemption must be manifested to men before
they can have any authority for approach unto Him,
or any desire so to do. Man may not only read, and
preach God as revealed in creation ; he may read and
preach God's will as revealed in natural law. For

13

herein that will is revealed, in that transgression of law brings punishment and obedience its reward. Yet proclaim as he may the truth herein made known, no salvation is wrought. The voices of nature may speak of God and law, but they cannot tell how one who has broken law and sinned against God may be restored to the divine favor. They cannot tell a guilty sinner of a way of approach to a mercy-seat. They may speak of an offended deity, but they cannot speak of a pardoning God. Do away with the knowledge that is given by inspiration of the Holy Spirit and you do away with the possibility of salvation. " The heavens are telling the glory of God and the firmament showeth his handiwork. Day unto day is gushing forth speech, and night unto night is whispering knowledge "; but vain preachers are they all to a guilty sinner. They exert no renewing powers upon his nature. It is only the law of the Lord which is perfect, that converteth the soul. The Holy Spirit in his word gives to man a true knowledge of self—a knowledge of self in relation to God—and above all he gives in that Book of books the knowledge of Jesus Christ. He tells the sinner of his sin and of a Saviour who is given specially for sinners. He tells men of their utter helplessness, and yet speaks to them of One who is able to save unto the uttermost all them that come unto God by him. He tells us that God in his justice has already condemned the sinner, and at the same time he tells us that God can be just and yet the justifier of him that believeth in Jesus. Thus he gives knowledge through the word which is able to save our souls through faith which is in Christ Jesus—knowledge by which the human agent in revival work is enabled to persuade men. Were this truth not given, revival work would be an impossibility. There can be no revival where there is no gospel. The sword of the Spirit is the word of God.

But the word of God given by inspiration of the Spirit has relation not only to the workers but to the subject operated upon in revival work. The knowledge of the truth is an indispensable pre-requisite to the acceptance of the Saviour. No one ever yet believed in Christ apart from the divine revelation concerning him. "How can they believe in him of whom they have not heard?" Man cannot exercise faith in that of which he is ignorant. The Saviour is given freely and fully for men, but he is presented solely for the acceptance of faith. Without faith Christ is no Saviour to any man. How then is that faith possible without which there is no salvation? "Faith cometh by hearing, hearing by the word of God." Thus the Holy Spirit's agency in giving the revealed truth which is able to save our souls is an indispensable element in all true revival work. There may be wild excitement, and there may be happy feeling resulting from mere human effort in religious work. Man—a naturally religious being—may be aroused, alarmed, and quieted again, yes, even rejoiced by the skilful swaying of his emotions, but unless men have been begotten by the word of truth, unless they have been begotten again, not of corruptible seed, but of incorruptible, through the word of God,

which liveth and abideth, they have no life in them.
They remain, even in their rejoicings over their fancied salvation, dead through trespasses and sins.   All
genuine revival must be effected through the proclamation and reception of the truth as it is in Jesus. Let
us then, in the first place, recognize the agency of the
Holy Spirit in revival work in that he has given to us
the word of God, without which revival work is an
impossibility.

*In the second place, we recognize the Holy Spirit's
agency in revival work as operating upon and exercised through the human agency employed.*

He dwells in his people, sanctifying them and fitting them for revival work.   He even gives desire by
which we are led to engage in such blest employ.   It
is he who wakens and inspires the prayer that calls
down the blessing.   It is he that draws forth that
service which is at the same time a result and a cause
of revival to those engaged in it, and those upon
whom it is exerted.   "He works in us both to will
and to do of his own good pleasure."   No man ever
yet was fitted to do such work for God, and no man
ever yet felt inclination to do such work for God apart
from the working of the Holy Spirit in him.   It is
only as we are led by the Spirit of God that we can
or do enter upon filial service.   The revival work that
is entered upon without his leading is spurious.   He
not only fits his people for this work by the renewing
and sanctifying of their natures, and by leading them
to consecrated service and fervent prayer; He oper-

ates on their minds with his enlightening power.  He
opens their understandings that they may understand
the Scriptures.  He guides his people into all the
truth.  "He takes of the things of Christ and reveals
them unto us."  Thus he gives, through the light
which he imparts through his truth, the necessary
knowledge by which the human agent in revival
work becomes a workman that needeth not to be
ashamed, rightly dividing the word of life.  Again,
he emboldens and empowers his people so that they
may speak the word of God with boldness.  No one
can think of a greater transformation in this respect
than that which took place in the lives and labors of
the apostles after they had received the promise of
the Father.  Then those men, craven-hearted, who
deserted their Lord in his agonies, charge home with
words of burning conviction the guilt of the death of
Christ upon their Jewish rulers.  Under the force of
a moral necessity they cannot but speak the things
which they have seen and heard.  Even he who
denied his Lord with curses because of his fear, when
accosted by a servant-girl, now boldly confronts the
very Sanhedrim of his people and charges home the
murder of God's Messiah upon them.  The unlettered
fishermen of Galilee fear not to stand in the temple
and preach unto the people all the words of this life.
What has so eminently fitted them for this great
revival work, where thousands under their preaching
are convicted and converted unto God ?  Here is the
simple answer to this question.  They are acting
under the Holy Spirit's agency.  Without this they

were even forbidden to work. "Behold, I send the promise of my Father upon you, but tarry ye in Jerusalem until ye be endued with power from on high. Ye shall receive power after that the Holy Ghost is come upon you." Thus, in all revival work, the power that makes men strong for service is the same. Men who are mighty for God labor under the power of his Spirit, strengthened with all might by his Spirit in the inner man. Even Christ himself was not in this respect an exception, but an example to his people. God gave not the Spirit by measure unto him, and as he enters on his mission after the temptation, this is the record of Scripture concerning him: "Jesus returned in the power of the Spirit into Galilee, and there went out a fame of him into all the region round about." The Spirit of the Lord God is upon me because he hath anointed me to preach the gospel. Then even Christ himself was fitted for his ministry.

But the Holy Spirit's agency is still further seen in the exercise of his power through his people's effort. His people may have zeal and knowledge and boldness, and yet all this must go for naught unless the Holy Spirit not only fits the worker for service, but afterward works through him. The Holy Spirit dwelling in his people exerts his power through their effort. In every awakening of religious enquiry, in every ingathering of souls, there are two exercises of power. The Holy Spirit is working, else God's people could do nothing, and God's people are working, else there is nothing done. God works and man works. Man works because God works in him. God works through man's working. Thus the words spoken in human weakness are yet spoken with the demonstration of the Spirit and with power. Thus it is that the gospel comes not in word only, but in power and in the Holy Ghost, and in much assurance. The Holy Spirit applies the truth with convicting and convincing power. It is he who makes the written word a living word. He in man speaks, speaks through man, speaks through man's speaking, speaks to man, and only as men hear his voice is salvation effected. Only through his agency is the agency of man successful. Not by might, not by power, but by my Spirit, saith the Lord. Thus is the weakness of human agency associated, interfused with the Spirit's mighty working. In the closest of all possible partnerships in labor we labor together with him. "We are laborers together with God." Thus the Holy Spirit works in and through his people for the conversion of men. Thus revival work becomes a possibility, and without him we can do nothing.

*In the third place, we would emphasize the Holy Spirit's agency in revival work in his immediate working on the hearts of the unregenerate, disposing them to receive the truth.*

It is his work not only to apply the word with power, but to prepare the heart for its reception. The regenerating influences of the Holy Spirit are exerted directly upon the human soul. He opens the heart to attend to the things that are spoken. It is by his

renewing power that the carnal mind, which is enmity against God, is brought to a loving acceptance
of the Saviour.    He so acts upon the heart that the
sinner who, if left to himself, would ever have gone
on rejecting the Christ, and hardening his heart, is
willingly constrained to embrace offered mercy.    Nor
is this constraint one that operates in antagonism to
the human will.    The Holy Spirit's agency, either
upon saint or sinner, is so subtle and so mysteriously
blended with the action of the human will, that man
is voluntarily active, even while acting under the
Spirit's control.    It is through the effectual working
of his mighty power that men are brought to the
obedience of faith, but his people are a willing people
in the day of his power.    Thus it is that the renewed
soul's activities, while truly human and truly volun-
tary, are at the same time the fruits of the Spirit.
" He works in us both to will and to do of his good
pleasure."    Repentance and faith are truly human
activities, but there never yet was genuine faith or
genuine repentance apart from the renewing power
of the Holy Ghost.    The manner of his operations in
his direct influence upon human hearts is to us unknown.    We know that he works, but we cannot tell
the way of the Spirit.    "The wind bloweth where it
listeth, and thou hearest the sound thereof, but canst
not tell whence it cometh or whither it goeth, so is
every one that is born of the Spirit."    Thus it is that
the indications of his presence and working are clearly
visible through the work of regeneration by which a
soul passes from death unto life, and which is deep in

the method of its operation beyond all human scrutiny. Yet, apart from this, his gracious working, no soul ever believed on the Lord Jesus Christ. The prophet may cry to the dry bones in the valley of vision, saying, " O ye dry bones, hear the word of the Lord "; but no flesh clothes them, no movement is felt or seen among them. How can these spiritually dead be quickened ? " Come from the four winds, O breath, and breathe upon these slain that they may live." Thus it is that they are made to live who were dead in trespasses and sins. This then is a third operation of the Spirit in revival working. Apart from this, his promised agency, all human working is in vain. In conjunction with this, his agency, he who preaches the gospel, though in weakness and in fear and in much trembling, will yet see the pleasure of the Lord prospering in his hand. We have not dwelt upon any special agency of the Holy Spirit, which is exclusively limited to revival work. We have spoken only of work that is evident in every case of individual conversion. We have done so because we believe that in stating the agency of the Holy Spirit in individual conversion, we state the agency employed in the greatest revival. The work is in its every feature the same in character or kind, the only difference is that of degree. He who is now in his people and in his churches is the same, and his work is the same in all human conversion. He gives the word, he enables his people to speak it, and he opens the heart for its reception.

## WORTHY IS THE LAMB.

Worthy is the Lamb that was slain.—Rev. v. 12.

A babe was born into our world in bitterest poverty.
His mother wrapped him in coarse scanty clothing and
laid him in a manger, because there was no room for
him in the inn. That child grew up despised and re-
jected and died amid shame and torment. That poor
babe of Bethlehem is now highest in heaven's honors.
His name is above every name. The greatest homage
that the universe of God can give is poured out before
him. A man may be praised in some little community
when he has but limited worth; an ordinary work of
art may win recognition in local competition, but it is
a very different thing to stand foremost and win highest renown in a world's exhibition. In higher worlds
than ours, Jesus Christ is praised. In a world's competition, one may be awarded foremost position in his
work and yet there may be diversity of opinion among
judges; but here, with the acclaim of creation, the pre-
eminent worth of Christ is celebrated. In exhibitions
of this world, one may win the prize, and yet others
may stand so close to him in merit as to deserve honorable mention. But here, no name, however worthy,
is associated with that of Christ. He alone is praised.
A man may borrow praise from inherited position.
The honors which are accorded to the Queen of England are gathered to her from the position which she
holds. Christ is praises for his inherent worth. Sometimes persons are led in ignorance to give praise to

one who, after all, may not much merit it. Here, as
the all-revealing light of heaven breaks upon character, and as highest and holiest intelligences behold
there is but one cry, Worthy is the Lamb. Sometimes
persons grow weary in sad satiety of that which once
was accounted most worthy, but here it is forever and
forever with increasing emphasis, Worthy is the Lamb.
Sometimes a party may be loud in the praises of its
favorite, and yet the object of that praise be as bit-
terly contemned by others; but here, every creature
which is in heaven and on earth and under the earth,
the assembled voices of the universe, all-impassioned,
proclaim him worthy of all that can be won by worth.
In every department he eminently leads. Worthy art
thou to receive blessing and honor and power and dominion and glory. Many a life may be judged worthy
of honor, but to be embalmed in the everlasting song
of one's country! So all-worthy is he of all honor and
power and glory, that there is no song in heaven like
the song that ascribes all honor to him. He has mag-
netized all heaven's hearts. Now, I ask a question:
Did Jesus Christ by that despised life on earth win
that honor which he now wears? How could one so
low rise so high? It is true that Jesus Christ is God
and as God is worshipped. Had he never undertaken
the work of man's redemption still heaven's adorations
were ever and would ever be his as the uncreated, all-
creating God. But the praise here offered to Christ
is gathered from his life on earth. The glory here
ascribed to him is to him not as uncreated God but as
the person who became man and died on Calvary

He is worshipped as the Lamb that was slain. Let us
look to-day at the Saviour's preëminent worth, whereby he is entitled above all others to this exalted homage.     The text says that he is worthy of all the
perferment which is given him.   Let us test the worth
of it by the laws of promotion which he has established in his own kingdom, and see if they do not
proclaim him entitled to the honors wherewith he is
crowned.   I ask no ground of promotion, no reasons
for perferment for the Redeemer other than the laws
of his own kingdom.   I ask not that any honor be
accorded to him for his divinity except as that
divinity is revealed in the worth of his redemptive
work. Let him be simply the Babe of Bethlehem, and
let him do what he has done and be what he has been,
and by the laws which determine all perferment in
his own kingdom Jesus Christ has won the transcendent honors which he wears. The Babe of Bethlehem,
the Man of Calvary, is not only highest in heaven's
honors but, judged by the laws of his own kingdom,
he is there by the preëminent worth of his own incarnate life.   Worthy is the Lamb that was slain.

Let us look to-day at the preëminent work of
Christ.   Judged by the laws of his own kingdom
Jesus Christ holds the throne of honor by transcen-
dent worth.

I. *It is a law of the kingdom (Christ has said) that
the honors conferred in it shall be according to work
done.*

(a) I will give unto every man according as his

work shall be. Man does not enter the kingdom by his works of righteousness, but the man who works righteousness in the kingdom finds reward, and reward proportionate to service rendered. He that can say, " Lord, thy pound hath gained ten pounds," shall hear his King and Judge say, " Have thou authority over ten cities." We may live life as if no such law existed. We may fritter away our possibilities thoughtless of that great law of the kingdom, but the law holds and operates all the same. We may be saved, yet saved with loss, and go empty-handed into the kingdom; be saved yet so as by fire, as a man that has lost all escaping barely with his life. The fire shall try every man's work of what sort it is. If any man's work abide which he hath built thereupon he shall receive a reward. If any man's work shall be burned he shall suffer loss. Yes, the law holds with inevitable sway : I will render to every man according to his works.

(b) Not only does the law exist, but it is eminently righteous. The man who, above all others, has rendered important service to his king and country, has reason to expect that merit shall meet with its appropriate reward. So much is this so that the honor of the throne and of the kingdom would be compromised if his claims were carelessly ignored. It was a righteous thing in Pharoah to take Joseph, the slave, from the dungeon, and place him second only to himself in the realm, when he rendered such service as none other could, such service as saved the whole realm from destructive famine. The monuments which nations uprear for their illustrious dead do not crown the graves of unworthy, aimless, indolent life, but of those who have won high achievement on the plains of war or in the arts of peace. Even nature's law is that reward must crown labor, and that if a man work not he must come to poverty. So the man who has wrought most for the kingdom, not necessarily the man who has been most conspicuous in its service, shall stand highest in the day of rewards. It is a righteous law that decrees that the faithful and unfaithful shall not be rewarded alike. Every one shall receive according to that he hath done. They that be wise shall shine as the brightness of the firmament, and they that turn many to righteousness as the stars for ever and ever.

(c) But if it is righteous that rewards should be proportionate to labor, Christ's work infinitely exceeds and transcends all other service.

How insignificant do all other works appear when compared with that which Christ has done! How vast and important beyond all conception must that work be which enfolds in its vast embrace even the universe of God, angels and men; that broke the power of sin in God's universe, accomplished eternal salvation for multitudes that no man can number, lifted them to untold heights of glory and eternal safety, and established all the holy forever in their sinless perfection — a work that, in its influences touches every creature and comprehends eternity.

Let all holy beings in heaven and on earth combine their power in effort to wipe out a single sin, and in their failure learn the value and the vastness of the work of him who beareth away the sin of the world. Let all strive to lift one soul from sin and its destruction, and in their failure learn the greatness of that work by which the vilest sinners of all ages and peoples are saved and presented faultless in glory.

A king may reign prosperously while there is no revolt of subjects in his realm, and his power is not known because it is not tested. But let unlawful and wicked rebellion rage, and the king, who not only subordinates all, but by a mighty triumph makes all future rising impossible—he out of this conflict shall achieve his highest glory. So Christ.

A king that can so overcome as to make revolting subjects his foremost allies, love-loyal even unto death for his honor,—he has honor out of his work. He that could go forth alone in an alien world, and engage all opposing powers, and get glorious victory in that highest conquest of love,—O how infinitely are all holy beings and all redeemed from among men indebted to the triumph he has won! If there is any child of God on earth striving to work righteousness, if there are saved sinners loving holiness now in heaven, it is all Christ's work. Among all the faithful who have conquered sin and who are now promoted to reign in glory, surely he is first who opened up the way for them, who conquered their own wills, and thus enabled them to pursue the right way, and then, by his power and grace, brought them off more than conquerors. Now, let Christ take the place of a subject under the laws of his own kingdom, and let the preferment be according to merit; if everyone is to receive according to that he hath done, then by the laws of that kingdom, the highest honors are evermore his due.    Worthy is the Lamb that was slain.

II. *It is a law of Christ's kingdom and of God's universe that character determines destiny.*

*(a)* The disclosures of the judgment of the last day reveal that it is grounded on character.    He that is righteous let him be righteous still, he that is filthy let him be filthy still.    This is true not only of the distinction between the righteous and the wicked, but however little or much our lives are controlled by the thought, it is true that the characters we as Christians are forming in this life and that we bear with us into the world to which we go, shall determine for us our position in the kingdom.    Character is certainly a condition of preferment in glory.    It is not the ground of their acceptance, but it is a condition of fulfilment. These shall walk with me in white, for they are worthy.    As one star differeth from another star in glory, so shall it also be in the resurrection.    Character certainly determines position in the kingdom.

*(b)* It is befitting in any kingdom that excellence of life should be a condition of preferment to positions of honor.    It is a disgrace to earthly governments, when besotted and vicious life is raised to positions of public trust.    It is the chiefest glory of nations when their rulers are men of righteousness, when the crown royal rests on the head of one who rules in righteousness, one who wears "the white flower of a blameless

life." But it is preëminently befitting that, in the kingdom of righteousness, character should be a condition of preferment. It would be a strange and anomalous thing if, in such a kingdom, a life of little personal worth should hold the reins of government. The ideal kingdom must have the ideal king.

(*c*) If then character can be and is a condition of preferment in the kingdom of redemption, think of the matchless worth of the character of Christ. Who is there that can compare with the Saviour? In every department of life he eminently leads. He passed through the moral contagion of this sinful world, where all had fallen 'neath its baneful power. He was tempted in all points like as we are, yet without sin. By the power of his holy life he became sin's destroyer. The severest tests that ever were applied to character were brought to bear upon him, and there is absolutely no flaw in his character—not the slightest fleck or stain. God is well pleased for his righteousness' sake. His hatred of sin and his love of holiness caused him to enter the very charnel-house of human sin, that he might wash it from its dismal stains in his own most precious blood. The wisdom and the power displayed in his atoning work have become the wonder of the universe and of eternity. He is the power of God and the wisdom of God. In him we have all the treasures of wisdom and knowledge. In him all glories meet. He is the chiefest among ten thousand, the altogether lovely. His righteousness is not simply superior to that of all others in the kingdom. They have all discarded their own

14

righteousness as a ground of acceptance and stand justified simply through his infinite merit.  O the transcendent and the unspeakable worth of Christ!

Now since character determines destiny, let the question be, Who is entitled by inherent worth to the exceeding honors connected with the kingdom of redemption?  Let every life be a privileged candidate.  Let Christ resign his native right to the throne and let the place of honor be awarded solely on the ground of merit.  Let the mighty angel cry aloud, Who is worthy to take the book and to loose the seals?  Who is worthy to rule in the kingdom of redemption?  Judged by the laws of his own kingdom, Christ alone is King.  No one in heaven or on earth or under the earth was found worthy to open the book or to look therein.  But see! there stands in the midst of the throne a Lamb as it had been slain.  Hear the acclaim of creation, Worthy is the Lamb that was slain to receive the honor and the power and the glory and the dominion and the blessing.

> Worthy thy hands to hold the keys,
>   Guided by wisdom and by love;
> Worthy to rule o'er mortal life,
>   O'er worlds below and worlds above.

Despised Galilean, by preëminent work thou hast won the throne.  Worthy is the Lamb that was slain.

III. *It is a law in Christ's kingdom that the life that is freest from self-seeking, nay, more, the life that can and does stoop lowest for others' good—the life of preeminent unselfishness—is the life that is fitted and destined for the highest exaltation.*

He that exalteth himself shall be abased and he
that humbleth himself shall be exalted.

(a) The world in which we live is a self-seeking
world. The effort of human life to-day is largely a
grasping of the good things for self, or an effort for
personal aggrandizement in the positions of promi-
nence and power. How many are the moves in all
departments of activity that have no higher motive
than selfishness. The world is full of selfishness. The
human heart is full of selfishness. "Look not every
man on his own things, but every man also on the
things of others" is a precept that is very little regarded in the conduct of life. Selfishness is the essential principle of the world's activity. Yet selfishness
is the essential principle of all sin. By this base
ambition to be chiefest Satan fell. By this setting
of self-will above the will of God man fell. To this
same principle of selfishness in the conduct of the
world's affairs the sorrow and suffering and wretch-
edness of the race are largely due. What principle
underlies the organized clashing of capital with labor
and of labor with capital? What is the spirit of mo-
nopolies and of chartered rights and protective tariffs?
Is it "Thou shalt love thy neighbor as thyself?" What
mean those walls of social separation between the more
and less favored members of society—those distinctions
which, though one in nature and operation with the
caste of the heathen, are also far from being outgrown
even within the charmed circle of church fellowship?
Is this the recognition of the principle that one is our
master, even Christ, and all we are brethren? Is this

that lowliness of mind that esteems others better than one's self ? Is this the fulfilment of that royal law, " As ye would that others should do unto you, do ye also even unto them " ? Or is it not in its spirit and action the very essence of selfishness ? This is simply the spirit of the world.

` (b) O how different is the law of life in the kingdom of redemption from that which sinfully obtains in worldly society ! Ye know that they which are accounted to rule over the Gentiles lord it over them, and their great ones exercise authority upon them. But it is not so among you ; but whosoever would be great among you shall be your servant, and whosoever would be first shall be servant of all. For verily the Son of Man came not to be ministered unto, but to minister and to give his life a ransom for many. Thus it is that the principle and the practice of unselfishness are fundamental in the kingdom of Jesus Christ. O what a kingdom that must be where every life is free from this great root of all evil ! But who is fitted to be king in such a kingdom as this ? The law of the kingdom says, He that is at the farthest remove from all self-seeking, he that can and does stoop lowest for others' good, he who stands foremost in the nobility of unselfish life, he is fitted and destined for this highest exaltation.

(c) Now let Jesus Christ stand divested of all native right, stand as one among all the creatures in God's universe, and let the question be, Who is worthy of this crown ? What life has most unselfishly fulfilled its mission ? Again let the mighty angel issue the challenge, " Who is worthy ?"

O was there ever unselfishness like to that which exchanged the throne of Godhead and the worship of all the holy for the manger of Bethlehem and the derision of sinners and the cross of Calvary? Jesus, being in the form of God, counted it not a prize to be on an equality with God, but he emptied himself taking the form of a servant, and being made in the likeness of men, and being found in fashion as a man, he humbled himself (infinite stoop!) and became obedient to death, even the death of the cross (O mightiest triumph of unselfish life!) Take the kingdom, O Christ, for thou hast won it by the triumph of unselfish life. It is done. Because of this God hath highly exalted him and given him a name that is above every name, that at the name of Jesus every knee shall bow. Worthy is the Lamb that was slain.

IV. *It is a law of Christ's kingdom that he who would aspire to any eminence in it, must be possessed of a mighty love—a love that can embrace even enemies.*

(*a*) How unnatural this is to the human breast! How the enmity of life kindles and burns when wrongfully entreated. What life-long feuds, what deadly hatreds, what wide-spreading animosities in the dark world, the ideal maxim of which was simply, "Thou shalt love thy neighbor and hate thine enemy." Even the twelve chosen disciples of Christ were slow to understand and yield obedience to a higher law. When the Samaritans refused to receive Christ as he journeyed through their country, the disciples hastily said, Lord, shall we command fire to come down from heaven and consume them, as Elias did? He simply answered: "Ye know not what spirit ye are of." Many a one who knows full well how to love a friend, knows not and dreams not of loving enemies.

(*b*) But the teaching of the principles of the kingdom is this: "Ye have heard that it hath been said, ·Thou shalt love thy neighbor and hate thine enemy,' but I say unto you, Love your enemies, bless them that curse you and pray for them that persecute you. For if ye love them which love you, what reward have ye? do not even the publicans the same?" Here is the law of the kingdom. The kingdom is itself a kingdom of love, its laws are love, and he who can come nearest to the fulfilment of its royal law must stand foremost in its honors.

(*c*) Let the highest honors of the highest kingdom be given according to the laws of the kingdom to him who merits them most. Let the crown of the kingdom be given, not by inheritance, but unto him, whoever he be, who is mightiest in love. Come forward, ye sons of light, care ye not for this crown? forward, ye that have basked in love from almost everlasting days! Nay! ye come not, ye blessed spirits. Ye know that there is no love like Immanuel's love. O love beyond degree, that brought the Saviour from the throne of the universe to the cross of shame! O love that ope'd thy side, in the face of blackest hate and didst give life-blood for enemies! O love infinite that hast bought thy church at such ransom to be thy bride!

"Jesus, thy boundless love to me
No thought can reach, no voice declare."

There is no love that can be brought into comparison
with this. Greater love hath no man than this, that
a man lay down his life for his friend ; but thou, O
Christ, hast laid down thy life for thine enemies. By
the laws of the kingdom, all honors belong to Christ,
for he has won them by the conquest of love. Worthy is the Lamb that was slain.

V. *It is a law of Christ's kingdom that suffering
and self-sacrifice for the kingdom of God's sake shall
be a condition of distinction in it.*

(a) When the two apostles in their childish strife
with their brethren as to which should be greatest,
came to Christ, saying, Grant that we may sit, one on
thy right hand and one on thy left in thy glory, He
asked them if they were able to fulfil the conditions
on the ground of which such preferment is secured.
Are ye able to suffer for this ? Are ye able to drink
of the cup that I drink of and to be baptized with the
baptism wherewith I am baptized ? If we suffer with
Christ we shall also be glorified with him. He that
saveth his life shall lose it, but he that loseth his life
for my sake, the same shall find it. The apostle speaks
in the 11th of Heb. of those who were tortured, not
accepting deliverance, that they might obtain a better
resurrection. Christ said, when enumerating the laws
of his kingdom, Blessed are ye when men shall revile
you and persecute you and say all manner of evil
against you falsely for my sake. Rejoice in that day

and be exceeding glad, for great is your reward in heaven. The shunned pathway of suffering is the pathway of promotion in Christ's kingdom.

*(b)* It is surely a righteous principle in government that they who have suffered most for the sake of the kingdom shall share most largely in its honors. Do we expect that the Christian who has shrunk from suffering and sacrifice for the cause of Christ, who has never given even of worldly goods without grudging, can take rank in the kingdom with apostles, prophets and martyrs who hazarded their lives for Jesus Christ ? While a Carey and Judson, a Timpany and Currie and McLaurin and their helpers gave themselves to lonely isolation, some to privation and suffering and death for the cause of Christ in distant lands, can the careless Christian, living in luxurious ease, expect such honor as they shall win, or such honor as shall be to those who, in the destitute parts of our own country, have given themselves to privation and almost beggary for the kingdom of God's sake ? Then · the principle is a righteous one, that they who have suffered most for the kingdom shall in it be honored most.

*(c)* Ye know the grace of our Lord Jesus Christ, how that though he was rich yet for your sakes he became poor. Never before and never again shall or can be such sacrifice as he made. He emptied himself of all the wealth of the universe, and when reduced to beggary his own great life was freely sacrificed for the kingdom's sake. Ye know the sufferings which he endured, nay, ye know them not ; ye know

of them only.   Prince of sufferers, Lamb of God for
sinners wounded, no one has begun to sacrifice or
suffer as thou hast done.   There are no burdens borne
like unto the burdens which thou didst bear for us.
There are no shame and indignity endured such as
that which was cast upon thee.   There is no death
like unto that which thou didst die.   To thy willing
sacrifice the kingdom owes all it is and all it evermore
can be.   If the law of the kingdom be that deepest
sacrifice and suffering for it shall win highest honor
and renown, then take the kingdom, for by preëmi-
nence in sacrifice and suffering it is justly thine own.
Worthy art thou to receive the power and riches and
wisdom and might and honor and glory and blessing,
for thou wast slain and didst purchase unto God with
thy blood men of every tribe and tongue and people
and nation.   Thus every law that operates in the
kingdom of redemption proclaims the transcendent
worth of Christ.   Among the kings of the nations
and the heirs of glory there is none that can be compared with him.   Let us rejoice in his courts and in
our homes to-day that such a King and Saviour is
ours.   Let us give to him the highest throne of honor
in our hearts and o'er our lives.   Let us take up
heaven's verdict even here on earth and make this
lost world vocal with the knowledge of the Saviour's
worth—with the passionate tenderness of love-loyal
life, let us take up even here redemption's song —
Worthy, worthy beyond expression and to eternity.
Worthy is the Lamb that was slain.

## THE UNEXPECTED WAY.

Look unto me and be ye saved, all the ends of the earth.
—Isaiah xlv : 32.

My thoughts are not your thoughts, neither are your ways my ways, saith the Lord.   For as the heavens are higher than the earth, so are my ways higher than your ways and my thoughts than your thoughts.   While thus the ways and the thoughts of God are so far above the thoughts and ways of mortals, it follows that man never can anticipate God in the outworkings of his purposes.   In pathways altogether unlooked for by mortals, he moves for the accomplishment of his unsearchable counsels.   God's thoughts are not our thoughts, and thus while man may be mapping out for himself ways in which he expects the Almighty to tread, he finds that God's ways are not his ways. Even expected blessing comes in most unexpected ways.   Man can never anticipate the Almighty.   Let us view this thought to-night, simply in reference to God's way of salvation as displayed in the verse before us.   While the way of human salvation is so simple and plain that the wayfaring man though a fool cannot err in reference to it, yet at the same time there is not a step in the whole redemption scheme which man could even have dreamed of before God revealed it to him.

*Let us view the unexpectedness of God's way of salvation as presented in the verse before us:* " Look unto me and be ye saved, all the ends of the earth for I am God."

I. *How unexpected to man is the source of human salvation.*

(*a*) Men never would have thought of looking to God as the source of their salvation  He was so great and so exalted, so far above all human affairs, that they never could have thought of him as one who would make them the objects of his special concern. He was occupied in the creation and controlling of unnumbered worlds ; how could he stop to make the little creature, man, the object of his special regard,— he before whom all heaven's angels bow, acknowledging their utter unworthiness in his presence ?  How then could a sinful creature, man, think that God would appear in his behalf ?  Rebelling angels who swerved from their allegiance to God's government, were never delivered by him : how then could man hope that God's mercy would be exercised in his behalf, when it was never thus exercised before ?  Nay, if God were such a being as man, he never would have interfered, and as men could only judge of him by themselves, they could never think of him as the source of their salvation.

(*b*) They never could have thought of salvation from such a source, for men were not only sinners and therefore abhorrent in God's sight, but they were sinners by breaking his holy law.  Men might look creation o'er to find some one who might propitiate God in their behalf ; but to think that the person against whom they had sinned should be the one to originate a way of mercy, this was most foreign to human thought.

Not only was their sin committed against God, but God himself was he that pronounced the sentence of death upon them because of sin.  But if he has thus passed sentence of death upon them, and he is the unchangeable one, how can man hope that salvation can originate with him ?  Nay, men might fear God and seek for salvation from his wrath, but how could they seek for salvation from that wrath in him alone whose wrath they feared ?

It was God's divine justice that cried for vengeance against human sin.  God's holy law declared, "the soul that sinneth it shall die."  God himself declared that not one jot or one tittle should in anywise pass from the law till all should be fulfilled.  The curse of God is thus upon man.  Where then shall man seek deliverance therefrom ?  Under such circumstances, would not mortals count him a raving madman who would counsel, saying, seek refuge from the wrath of God in God himself, whose wrath burns like a consuming fire ?  Would not human counsel run in the very opposite direction ?  If there be anywhere in the universe of God where a creature can find absence from God, then seek that place as a refuge from his wrath.  Yes, this would be the highest human conception of a possible way of salvation.  This is man's way and man's thought.  Now when the words of God break in upon man, do they not reveal an unexpected source of salvation ?  Sinner, crying, whither shall I go from thy Spirit, and whither shall I flee from thy presence ? listen, hear, and you shall live : *Look unto me and be ye saved, for I am God.*  Man might say : Nay, thou art God, and I have sinned, therefore thou art my destruction. God says ; I am God and thou hast sinned, therefore I am thy salvation. Look unto me and be ye saved, for I am God.

(c) Men never would have thought of God as the source of their salvation, for all had formed false conceptions of God's thoughts concerning them. They thought that God hated them for their rebellion against him. They knew that as judge he had condemned but they did not know his fatherly pity. They hated God and knew that he knew it, and therefore they thought that he hated them. They never had even asked God for salvation, and never of themselves would humble themselves to ask it of him, and he is the great God whom man has offended. How then can he lay his anger by while man's hate and pride and sin are unsubdued, while man will not even submit to ask God for his salvation. While man continues sinning, and while God says the soul that sinneth it shall die, how can God save ? God would be the most unexpected source of salvation to man in the whole universe. Yet to man's inquiry after a way of salvation—yes the voice of God to man preceding such inquiry—is, Look unto me and be ye saved for I am God.

II. *But not only is the source of salvation an unexpected one, the kind of salvation is one so utterly unexpected that faith itself is unable to grasp its vastness even after it has been declared.*

(a) Think of it, that God should not only save a

guilty rebel but that the salvation wherewith he
saved him should be of such a kind that the creature
should be unspeakably better off than before he fell !
The redeemed of a fallen race are raised to a far
higher glory than ever Adam possessed in his prime-
val innocency.   Rebel sinners are brought from the
depth's of sin's degradation not simply to enjoy an
earthly paradise but to enter heaven itself and there
to stand  conspicuous among  the armies of  light,
crowned as conquerors with Christ in his glorious
victory, made kings and priests unto God to reign
forever and ever, to be the living temples of the Holy
Spirit, to be transformed into the image of God's own
Son, to be honored beyond all others by Christ in that
he assumes human nature and even wears it in honor
of redeemed humanity, to be made such special objects
of the unspeakable love of God that even angels
are to learn the most they are to know of God's
Christ from the exhibitions of grace and love given
to fallen man.   There is no creature even in heaven
so honored as redeemed humanity.  Tell me, is not
this an unexpected kind of salvation ?  If human
thought had labored till reason reeled in its citadel
could it ever have imagined such a salvation as this ?
Nay, from the beginning of the world men have not
heard nor perceived by the ear, neither hath eye
seen, O God, beside thine, what he hath prepared for
sinners saved by grace.

    (d) Still further that he should not only so unspeak-
ably exalt and bless, but that he should place the creature thus blessed forever beyond the reach of any such

disaster as that by which he previously fell. Man in Edenic probation lived simply day by day by a tested obedience of his own, and failing once in that obedience forfeited forever his right to divine favor. Man redeemed stands no longer on the chance-work of his own efforts. He is not simply reinstated in the position occupied prior to the fall and to try a second chance of life through an attempt to render a perfect obedience. His final salvation is already secured through the finished work, the perfect obedience of Jesus Christ. The salvation of the true believer is made as certain and as eternal as the life of God. Because I live, ye shall live also: I give unto them eternal life and they shall never perish. Not only that life should thus be forever secured, but that a progressive work of sanctification should be carried on in each one till at last all shall stand holy and blameless before him in love, to stand forever established in holiness, an elect race, a royal priesthood, an holy nation, a people for God's own possession, that ye might thenceforth know the excellences of him who hath called you out of darkness into his marvellous light. O how meagre and how paltry are men's ideas of salvation compared with that of God! Men talk about annihilation, about cessation of conscious suffering. Yes, this is the most golden dream that mere human thought can devise concerning a future state and deliverance from the curse of sin; salvation by extinction, the promise of eternal but unconscious vacancy and dreamless death. It hath not entered into the heart of man to conceive the things which God hath prepared for them that love him. From all such vain philosophies and empty dreamings God bids the dying sinner turn his eyes: Look unto me and be ye saved, all ye ends of the earth, for I am God and beside me there is none else.

III. *In the third place, how unexpected is the way or method which God has provided and presented for human salvation.*

*(a)* The universe of God might have been challenged, but neither man nor angel could have guessed the way of salvation, that God himself—in Christ—should take upon him the sinner's guilt and make expiation for it through the suffering of death, and then bid the sinner look unto him and see his salvation thus effected; that Christ should become incarnate, the manifested God, that men might behold him; that he should make his soul an offering for sin and render in his own person complete satisfaction to broken law, and then bid a sinner look and see his full salvation perfectly secured in the atoning work of Calvary! Look unto me all the ends of the earth and be ye saved, for I am God. Now tell me, could mortal thought have ever guessed such a plan of salvation: that God should assume human nature, that he should humble himself, and, as God-man, become obedient unto death, even the death of the cross, and through that death open up a way of life for guilty man! O wonder of wonders! O unexpected way of salvation!

> Lord, shall our grief or joy prevail?
>   Our hearts are rent amidst the strife;
> Shall we the victim's death bewail?
>   Or hail it as the way to life?

This way of life is so utterly unexpected, that men are not ready, not able to believe it, even when told.

(*b*) No one would ever have thought that human works would have no factor in human salvation. God's way is so entirely different from all preconceived human opinion, that, even when seeking souls profess to be coming to God in his own way, they are mistaken, by introducing ways and methods of their own. The first effort of every soul that enters the kingdom is to work for its own salvation, and it ceases not so to do until it finds proof of the worthlessness and fruitlessness of self's doings in a bitter experience of unsuccessful endeavor. Even while Christ proclaims from the cross, It is finished, men go about to add their own doings to a Saviour's finished righteousness, and add the polluted patchwork of their own self-righteousness to the sacred completeness of the stainless robe of Christ. How difficult it is, even for Christians who have entered the kingdom, to disabuse their minds of these false theories of the way of life, even while the heart may have accepted Christ as the only Saviour. Half of Christendom failing to comprehend the vastness and freeness of gospel grace are yet found proclaiming a salvation partly by faith and partly by works, and this even in the very face of Scripture statement: that it is not of works, lest any man should boast; but by grace are ye saved through faith, and that not of yourselves, it is the gift of God. The apostle argues that salvation must either be exclusively by works or exclusively by grace, that it cannot be an intermixture of both. If it be by

15

works, then it is no more of grace, otherwise grace is
no more grace; and if it be by grace, it is no more of
works, otherwise work is no more work. The fact
that a man must be saved before he can perform any
God-accepted service, is proof that God's way of salvation is solely by grace. Yet, so foreign are God's
ways from man's ways and his thoughts from man's
thoughts, that men can scarcely be brought to believe
the repeated statement of Scripture, that salvation is
a free gift. God's way is an unexpected way of life.
That salvation should be obtained simply by looking
with the eye of faith to God—not by doing, but by
looking — is that which confounds human reason.
Such a gospel is to the Jew a stumbling-block and to
the Greek foolishness. Yet this and this only is the
God-appointed way of life. There is life in a look at
the crucified one. As Moses lifted up the serpent in
the wilderness, even so must the Son of Man be lifted
up, that whosoever believeth in him should not perish,
but have everlasting life. Look unto me all the ends
of the earth and be ye saved, for I am God.

IV. *God's salvation is unexpected to man in the
time in which it is effected.*

(*a*) God's salvation is effected instantaneously
through looking. Look and in looking be saved.
Saved by looking at a work already done ? Yes, and
saved even while thus you look. Now this is so
different from man's way, so foreign to all human
thought concerning the great salvation, that unsaved
ones here to-night are not ready to believe that even

now, by a look of faith, a dying sinner may pass from death unto life. Man's thought is that there must be a long time of self-preparation before sinners can come to God. God says man cannot begin to prepare until first he comes to God, and that therefore his only hope is to look away from self at once and forever, to God as a source of salvation. Man plans, saying, I must do this and that, I must feel this and that; God says nothing about doing and feeling as a means of salvation. He says, Look unto me and be saved. God's way is not man's way. You may think that salvation is not an instantaneous act, that a man attains to it only through many days and months of toil; and you may spend days and months of anxious toil in seeking salvation and at the end be no more saved than when you began; but the moment you look by faith to Christ, that moment you are saved, passing from death to life at his call. Not merely a future hope, but a present salvation. Verily, verily, I say unto thee, he that heareth my word and believeth on him that sent me, hath everlasting life and shall not come into condemnation, but is passed from death unto life. A present blessing, not merely a promise to be fulfilled at the close of life.

(b) Not only instantaneous, but carrying with it the conviction of present certainty. Men who profess to have accepted Christ as the great salvation, yet often are heard to say, that you cannot be certain of your salvation till you get past this present life. Yet God pledges present salvation to him who looks

by faith to Christ.   Look unto me and be ye saved,
for I am God.

> I hear the words of love,
>   I gaze upon the blood,
> I see the mighty sacrifice
>   And I have peace with God.

V. *Again God's salvation is unexpected in the universality of its offer, Look unto me all the ends of the
earth and be ye saved.*

(*a*) He fixes no geographical boundaries beyond
which the gospel message may not pass.  All the ends
of the earth are invited to look to him, and all the
ends of the earth shall see the salvation of our God.
How different is this, God's gracious purpose, from all
the narrow preconceptions of men.   The Jew in the
exclusiveness of his national religion could not think
of the Gentile as being partaker with him of the
same benefits.   It was a mystery that had been hid
for ages, that the Gentiles should be fellow-heirs and
of the same body, and partakers of the promise in
Christ by the gospel.   How difficult it was for even
the apostles to comprehend the full scope of the great
commission, that common salvation was to be preached
to every creature.   All nations were to be blessed in
him.   All the ends of the earth were to see the salvation of our God.   Yet this was so different from nar-
rowing national prejudices that Christians had to be
driven by persecution from Judea in order that they
might thus be made to preach among the heathen the
unsearchable riches of Christ.   Yes, and when these
heathen looked unto God from all the ends of the

earth and were saved, even an apostle wondered at the marvel of grace so far outreaching and transcending all human thought. Astonished when the great fact of not simply a national but a world's salvation dawned unto them they exclaimed, Then hath God granted unto the .Gentiles also repentance unto life! Yes, the great salvation was unexpected in the universality of its offer embracing every creature, all the ends of the earth in its universal call.

(b) In another sense was its universality unexpected. God excluded none from the offer of the gospel because of the vileness of personal character. The proud Pharisee who looked upon himself as exclusively the favorite of heaven might draw closely around him the garments of his self-righteousness, lest he should come in contact with the publicans and sinners of his day. Yes, this is man's idea. His offer of salvation would be based on excellency of personal character, and since salvation is a salvation from sin he would thus exclude from it those who need it most. God says, Go ye into all the world and preach the gospel to every creature. Does not even the Christian of to-day sometimes shrink from declaring the gospel to the most abandoned of the vile? O let us learn and act upon the unexpected breadth of God's great salvation! Let every creature in the habitable globe be assured that, however unworthy, he is embraced in the world-wide invitation of our God. Look unto me all the ends of the earth and be ye saved, for I am God.

Now, unconverted soul, whatever be your state or

place, are you not included in this offer. This world-wide call of mercy comes this night to you.

(*c*) Does not this way of salvation, so priceless, so easy, place eternal life within your reach however poor or helpless you may be ? If you cannot do anything, if you cannot pay anything, can you not look unto God ? This is the simple condition on which your salvation rests : Look unto me and be ye saved.

(*d*) Does not this present opportunity, while God is calling to you from his word, make it possible to look to Christ and be saved ?

> There is life in a look at the crucified One,
>     There is life at this moment for thee,
> Then look sinner look unto Him and be saved,
>     Unto Him who was nailed to the tree.

Look unto me all the ends of the earth and be ye saved, for I am God and beside me there is none else.

# POETICAL PIECES.

### A REVERIE.

A weary day of unsuccessful toil, departing with its sad and
    changeless record,
Was moving through the cloud-crowned gates of evening
    to the eternal past,
The glaring sun slow-sinking in the folds of western cloud
    was lost,
And twilight's gathering shadows deepened into darkness.
For him who is not blinded by the veil of commonness,
    departing day
Hath awful glories.   Oh how much of beauty dwells behind
    time-woven curtains ?
I had gazed upon the changing splendors as they rose before
    me,
Grasping for something vaster, all forgetful of my littleness,
When like an Alpine torrent thought rolled back on self,
And in the darkness of that lonely hour I felt my nothing-
    ness.
One of the countless myriads of things who dwell upon an
    atom,
Poised in boundless space, 'mid worlds innumerable,
Incapable to move to other spheres, incapable to know my-
    self or aught beside ;

Thus ran my thoughts, and then I think I justly spake
　　against my kind :
Oh man of science ! scientific worm, circling around a little
　　spot of dust,
Boasting of knowledge, prating of what thou knowest, send-
　　ing thy boastful breath abroad,
Asserting that there is no God in heaven, or, if there be,
　　that thou
Hast proved His Word untrue by thy far-reaching wisdom,
Who art thou, vile thing of weakness, that in thy presump-
　　tuous folly dar'st to sit
In judgment, and condemn as false the words of Him,
Who, throned above the rolling spheres, is Ruler over all,
And God of truth ?　Who art thou, replying against thy
　　Maker ?
Asserting, on thy veritable knowledge, that He lays false
　　claim
To thy creation.
Here, again, in viewing littleness in others I forgot myself,
And grew to fancied greatness.　Then again the tide of
　　thought
Roll'd back on self, with memory of the day's defeats,
And suffering from comparison e'en with those who toiled
　　together with me,
Feeling how much of all things must remain unknown to
　　all,
How much of all that's knowable unknown to me,
Who scarce can grasp the little sands that lie upon the
　　boundless beach
Of knowledge.
Then the conscious cry of weakness rising up within me
Died in weakness, and I said : Lord, what is man that
　　Thou

Art mindful of him? What the son of man that Thou
  should'st visit him?
Father, I bless Thee that Thou dost descend to dwell with
  men.
Father! What word is this I breathe? Am I His child?
Then I am born for endless years and glorious destiny;
Joined by the closest bonds to perfect life and noblest being,
Nor all created things can make a boast like mine.
Oh, mystery! myself am veriest littleness, yet incomparable
  greatness,
And through the consciousness of littleness is this greatness
  known.

---

## QUEEN ESTHER.

The festal days are come in Persia's royal halls,
  The glittering court is filled with noble peers,
There's revelry of joy; mirth loud and louder calls,
  But captive Israel answers back through tears.

Still swells the feast convivial; orient wealth is strewn,
  And royal wine is poured from golden bowls;
The light corruscant blazes, and the lofty dome
  Mirrors its splendors as the scene unrolls.

The king in regal state parades his glorious power,
  And Persia's courtiers quaff the foaming wine.
But see! another cup is mingled in this hour;
  O captive Israel, draughts of death are thine.

The subtle son of Agag gains the dread degree,
  The seal irrevocable marks the doom;
The race of captives blotted from the earth shall be,
  And naught may change the fiat of the throne.

From Persia's broad realm ascends a bitter cry,
    A death-doomed people prays and fasts in tears ;
The fervent prayer is heard by Him who rules on high,
    The star of hope, on sorrow's night appears.

A youthful exile, frail, yet fair as morning light,
    A daughter of captivity, is Persia's queen,
And queen through peerless beauty: in her beauty bright
    Fairest of all that royal halls have seen.

Hadassa, Esther, from the height of matchless charms,
    With royal crown and Persia's highest praise,
Views her despised people in their last alarms,
    Then looks on death, and ventures life to save.

"They live not, who approach the king, except he call,
    Not even Vashti might transgress his word,
Yet I will go unto the king, what'er befall,
    E'en though I perish.   Pray ye to the Lord."

O Israel, fervent be thy prayers, for see, her form
    Is trembling, and she moves with quickening breath ;
Like some lone bird on weary wing, against the storm,
    She presses on, and enters.   Is it death ?

Like a fair lily, see she stands before the throne,
    The extended sceptre hails her welcome guest,
But now the crisis past, white as the ocean's foam,
    Breathless she sinks ere heard in her request.

She wakes, the palace swims before her dreamy sight,
    But fears are flown ; it is the king's own hand
And voice that comfort : " Ask all thy delight,
    For half my kingdom is at thy command."

Soon the request is made ; she hears with gladdening thrill,
  " Thy people and thy foes I give to thee,
Take this reverseless seal, and write ye what ye will."
  Tis done ; her people now are free, are free.

O, Israel, ne'er forget deliverance so sweet,
  As turned death-darkness into joy-crowned days,
And unto Him, to whom your highest thanks are meet,
  In glad remembrance chant Queen Esther's praise.

---

### WILD FLOWERS.

Sweet little gems that deck earth's rugged brow,
When first to gentle spring bleak winter yields,
No kindly hand your tender beauty shields,
And yet ere verdure clothes the cultured fields,
Ye bloom on mountain cold, and valley low.

How strange, the woodland chill should be your home !
That ye should blossom in a lonely wild !
That craggy rocks in wild confusion piled,
Should be a home for Nature's tenderest child—
Ye forest beauties on your mountain throne !

I've seen you when mid storm and tempest wild
Ye bowed and fell, with leaves all rent and torn,
And thought how I adversity had borne :
My heart drank in the blackness of the storm :
Ye, crushed to earth, looked up again and smiled.

Your little lives so pure are not in vain,
Your tender forms in stainless beauty drest,
Your calm repose, amid the world's unrest,
Are words by which God hath Himself express'd,
And leads the seeking mind to Him again.

Fair family of God, your loving forms
Make deserts like to Eden's blissful bowers ;
In deep ravines and over mould'ring towers
Your beauty shines, like sunbeams, 'mid the showers,
Like wreaths of rainbow, 'mid the frown of storms.

Choice leaves in nature's volume, in the hours
Of converse with you, the rapt soul ascending,
With thoughts of you and the hereafter blending,
Looks up to yon bright world of bliss unending,
With the sweet prospect of unwithering flowers.

---

## ALBUM VERSES.

Choose thou the light, the pure and holy light—Jno. xii: 36.
And in God's light thou light shalt clearly see—Ps. xxxvi : 9.
Live in the light, a child of day and light—Thess. v : 5.
And ever growing light thy path of light shall be—Prv. iv : 18.
Let shine your light, the world-illuming light—Matt. v : 16.
And Christ who is the light shall shine on thee—Eph. v : 14.
Walk in the light as He is in the light—1 John i : 7.
And evermore His light thy light shall be—Rev. xxii : 5.

Serious thoughts are sometimes seen in merry faces,
    Sadness often looks from laughter lighted eyes ;
Naughty guests could never have such pretty dwelling
        places,
    So I guess they're angels coaxing to the skies.

————

The darkest night ne'er kept the dawning day
    From gaining noonday brightness in the heights above ;
Nor can beclouding fears keep back faith's morning ray
    From gaining light effulgent in the life of love.